Rose was born in Burnham, Berkshire, married her late husband Joe at 18 and has two daughters. Family is everything, so be thankful for what you have even if it's not perfect.

Rose Tierney

DANCING IN THE DARK

AUSTIN MACAULEY PUBLISHERS™

LONDON • CAMBRIDGE • NEW YORK • SHARJAH

A CIP catalogue record for this title is available from the British Library.

ISBN 9781035821426 (Paperback)
ISBN 9781035821433 (ePub e-book)

www.austinmacauley.com

First Published 2023
Austin Macauley Publishers Ltd®
1 Canada Square
Canary Wharf
London
E14 5AA

Thanks to all my family (Lisa, Sharon, Aoife and Max) for their encouragement. To Niamh, who was first to read a few chapters and told me it was good and to finish it. Ava for always looking out for me and for making me smile. To Gearoid (RIP) for all your quirky sayings, and to Joe (RIP) for being my one true love.

1

Joey

Here I am all wound up, waiting for the post. It always used to come by 10 am but it's now 10:30. Monday A-level results day! Gotta say didn't think I would be this nervous. I know I've done all the graft and found the exam papers kind of okay and everyone says I'm going to ace it.

No pressure but there's always that thought in the back of my mind; don't be stupid you passed, I told myself. It's like this I have to pass four good A grades then I'm off to university.

Positive thinking, I'm telling myself, be confident but it's not working!

God, where's the postman? I'm now at the living room window looking for Postman Pat's little red van. God, these net curtains need washing, didn't notice that before.

Mum was the only one who kept everything clean and tidy and since she died, Dad kinda does the best he can but to be fair, neither me nor my brother Eamon do too much cleaning, well not to Mum's standards.

JESUS CHRIST! Where's that bloody postie! I bet he knows he's got everyone's results and he's thinking, *I'll make them sweat*. It's mad, one sheet of paper is going to change my life, not just my life; once I pay off my student loan and get a decent job, I can help my family and Dad won't have to work so hard just to keep us bobbing along.

We've never had a holiday abroad. The only place we go is to Ireland where Dad is from, not that I don't like it there. I actually have always loved it, myself and Eamon had so much freedom there when we were younger.

My grandparents are great. They used to live on an island in Connemara but now live on the mainland as they are getting older.

I need to pass my exams. I need to pass. Please let it be okay. Joey, I tell myself, stop worrying. You've passed. Keep telling myself that! This is nuts. I need something to occupy my mind, something, anything to take my thoughts off—

The doorbell rings. I run to the door and throw it open, eager for my results.

It wasn't the postman.

It was Amy.

We are standing there staring at each other. And it takes me a couple of seconds to realise she's not on her own. I'm looking down into a buggy with a baby.

"Hello Joey."

I haven't said a word. The baby in the buggy has my full attention.

"Can I come in?"

"Er sure, of course." I step back to let her in. Amy wheels the buggy past me. I closed the door frowning. She stands in the hallway biting her bottom lip, she's watching me but saying nothing.

"Go through." I indicate the open door into the sitting room. I follow her in, I'm thinking what is she doing here? I haven't seen her in—it had to be well over a year and a half. What did she want?

"Are you babysitting?" I point to the baby in the buggy.

"Yeah, you could say that," Amy says, looking around the room stopping at the many family photos, Dad was always taking photos but stopped when we lost Mum and he hasn't picked up his camera since.

She keeps studying each photo. To be honest, I don't see what's so interesting. While she's studying the photos, I'm studying her. She looks the same maybe a bit slimmer, she's dressed in a pair of faded Levi 501s and a light blue T-shirt with a black jacket lying across the buggy handles.

Her blonde hair is a little longer than last time I saw her. But she's still stunning with big brown eyes. I look down at the buggy and the bundle is staring up, fascinated at the light fitting.

"What's its name?"

"Her name is Rosie, d'you wanna hold her?"

"No, I mean no, thank you." Was Amy mental or what? No way did I want to hold a baby. And she still hasn't said why she's here. I mean I am pleased to see her, it's just been such a long time.

Amy had dropped out of school, it must be over 18 months ago and I haven't seen or heard from her till today. And now she's standing in my house.

It's like she knows what I'm thinking as she says, "I went away to live with my aunt and I'm just back today visiting a friend and thought I'd look you up as well and say hi. I hope you don't mind?"

I shook my head, plastering a smile on my face and feeling strangely awkward.

9

"I'm going away today actually," Amy continued, "I'm going to Wales to stay with friends for a while."

"That's nice," I reply. "Can I get you a drink?" I say at last.

"Some water would be good, thanks." I head back from the kitchen with a glass of water and hand it to Amy. Her handshakes slightly as she drinks and then she puts the glass down.

She retrieves the cigarette from her jacket pocket and lights it up, saying, "do you mind if I smoke?"

"Well, I don't mind but my Dad and Eamon are very anti-smoking and they will be back soon."

"How soon?" asks Amy urgently.

I shrugged, "half hour or so."

God, Dad and Eamon will do their nuts if they smell smoke.

I'm looking at her, wondering what to say now. "So what've you been up to?" I ask.

"Looking after Rosie," replies Amy.

Silence again.

Thankfully, the baby starts gurgling, "what about you?" Amy asks as she picks the baby from the buggy. "What have you been up to?" She's not looking at me as she speaks, she is looking into the face of the thing wiggling in her arms. For the first time since she's arrived, she looks at me and asks how my A-levels went.

"I'm actually waiting for my results today," and hopefully, fingers crossed, it goes okay. "Anyway Amy, whose baby is she?" And then at that moment, the baby starts crying, well not crying, bawling so bloody loud.

PAPILLONS

Best 100 cu

best queer cgqzcu

HIPS 10%

Holetown, Barbados

"Her nappy needs changing," says Amy, "hold her for a second, I need to get her stuff out," she thrust the baby at me and I have no choice but to take her.

I'm holding the baby at arm's length, she stinks and I'm trying to put as much distance between me and her. Amy opens a blue bag and removes a baby mat decorated with unicorns.

She lays it down on the floor, smoothing it out, next comes a disposable nappy, a pink plastic bag and some baby wipes and with a small smile, she takes the baby from me, thank god!

I open the window to try and get rid of the smell as Amy kneels down and seems happy to deal with the poo, as she chats away to the stinky thing on the mat. I think I might get sick. "You should watch this," Amy says, "you might learn something."

Yeah right, I think. Amy puts the stinky overflowing nappy in the pink plastic bag and ties the top. "See Joey, it's very simple, even you could do it."

"Yes but why would I want to, Amy?" then she goes to hand me the plastic bag with the dirty nappy in it. "No fucking way, Amy."

"For God sake, Joey, poo or baby?" I take the bag from Amy and run to the bin with it at arm's length. I can hear Amy laughing and when I came back into the room, she is still laughing and smiling at me; she finds it very amusing.

Her smile brings back memories I've buried somewhere and Amy still hasn't told me why she's here. I'll try again. "Amy, why are you here?"

"Shush, she's falling asleep," Amy whispers as she places the baby back in the buggy. "Here Joe, look at this," as she handed me an envelope. I open the envelope and inside is a birth certificate, it says the child's name and the mother's name is Amy.

But there is no name for a father. I'm staring at her. "You are the baby's mother?"

She nods. "Joey, I need to tell you something."

Amy isn't even 19 yet and she's had a baby! How could she be so stupid to have a kid at her age? Had she never heard of the pill? Babies are for people in the 30s not our age.

2
Joey

"Joey, are you listening?"

"Huh?" I am trying to wrap my head round the fact that Amy is a mum.

Amy is looking at me as she takes a deep breath and says, "Joey, you're the dad, Rosie is our daughter." I feel like I've been hit by a truck, I'm looking at Amy, looking for an expression or a smile to tell me she's just joking.

I can't speak, my legs feel like jelly. I collapse onto a chair. My heart is pounding. I'm looking at her waiting for her to take back these words, it just can't be true. She's going to say I'm joking and laugh at me; please Amy, say it.

But she doesn't say anything. This isn't true, it can't be true, my stomach is heaving, my head is pounding. I start to remember things I don't want to remember. That night at Luca's party almost 2 years ago, how I drank far too much that night but then so had Amy, so had everyone.

It was sometime after Christmas. Amy bought me aftershave even though we were only going out a couple of months. I bought her some silver earrings as I didn't have much money.

We laughed and exchanged gifts then we danced and kissed and danced more and snogged and danced and danced and drank and kissed, then someone said get a room so we did; we went upstairs and found a room, we started kissing more, it was the first time for both of us and the whole thing was over nearly before it started. So how come one quick encounter makes a baby, a child, my child, no no no.

"I don't believe you, my name is not on the birth certificate, you're a liar! You're just looking for someone to blame and thought of me, how can you know that that thing is mine?"

3

Amy

Amy's face hardens and if looks could kill, I would be dead. "I don't sleep around, Joey, plus I have never been with anyone but you and if you say that again, I'm gonna thump you; for your information, I didn't put your name on the birth certificate because you had to be with me otherwise it's not allowed. I didn't come here to argue with you. I just came here to tell you."

"Then why did you come, Amy, just to upset me, to wind me up?"

"Joey, I thought you had a right to know."

"You come here, Amy, and throw a grenade into my world, how come you didn't just have an abortion?"

"Because Joey, I was living with my mum but she kicked me out, so I had to go live with my aunt but because she is a Catholic, abortion was out of the question and my aunt made it clear now she doesn't want me and the baby around."

"Well Amy, you should've had it adopted then."

"So, you think this is all my fault, Joey, I didn't make Rosie all on my own, did I?"

"No no, sorry Amy, it's just I can't get my head round all this."

"To be honest, Joey, I took one look at Rosie and fell in love; there was no way I could give her up for adoption and stop calling her 'it'; her name is Rosie."

"You should've told me, Amy."

"Why, what would you have done, Joey?"

"I don't know, sorry but you shouldn't have gone through this on your own."

"Joey, I'm going to Wales to make a new life. I've got a place to live there," she glanced down at her watch. "Joey, could you do me a favour?"

"What?"

"Could you look after Rosie for a little while? I need to pop to the shops and buy some nappies and other stuff."

"Hell no! Why can't you take it with you?"

"Stop calling her 'it'. Rosie doesn't like being moved around when she's just fallen asleep, she'll wake up and cry the place down."

My mind is spinning, this can't be real. I don't know what to do or say! I'm shaking my head. "Please Joey, I'll be back before Rosie wakes up, she'll sleep now for at least a couple of hours."

"Amy, please! If she wakes up, I wouldn't have a clue what to do."

"Joe, you don't have to do anything. I'll be back in about 20 minutes, 30 minutes tops, okay." Amy is already gone out of the sitting room towards the front door.

"Amy, no way are you leaving her with me, I can't do this, I don't know how to do this and I'm going out soon anyway."

"Joey you're not going out yet, you're waiting for your exam results."

"Amy, no! You can't leave your baby here."

"She's your baby too, Joey." And with that she's out the door and walking along the pavement, each step that took her further away, the more my stomach got tied in knots. I just wanted to go back to bed and start this day again, why is this happening to me? I have a daughter, a daughter called Rosie; oh God, help me!

My phone pings, it's my girlfriend Zoe asking me about my exam results. The doorbell rings, thank God Amy has come back. I open the door.

"Hiya, got a package for your Dad that needs signing for and some other letters, one I think you might be waiting for," the postman said smiling.

I signed for something in a daze and the top envelope is addressed to me; shutting the front door, I lean against it. Then slide down the door onto the floor, I'm staying here. I'm scared to go into the sitting room where she is.

I tear open my envelope on autopilot, my exam results. I feel ice cold and very alone, I want to cry, I look down and unfold the letter; four A stars.

In the sitting room, the baby starts to cry.

4

Joey

I look into the buggy and see the scrunched up face and tears flowing down its cheeks, it's watching me and I'm watching her, I feel like crying with her. The baby cries and cries and then cries some more and I just want to join in but I can't because boys don't cry and I can hear my dad's voice in my head telling me to man up, hold it together.

It's crying still, 2 minutes, 5 minutes turns to 10 minutes and it's getting louder and louder! I've gotta get out of this room, otherwise my head is going to explode; jumping to my feet, I leave the room closing the door behind me.

I go to the kitchen, pour myself a cold glass of water, where the hell is Amy? She's been gone over 20 minutes. The noise in the sitting room is still going on. I'm pacing up and down the hall realising my whole world is dissolving around me.

Keep it together Joey, Amy will be back soon, keep calm, breathe, I tell myself. Amy will be back soon and she'll take the baby away to Wales and no one would even know that she and the baby had ever been here.

Then I can get on with my life and she can get on with hers. I've walked up and down this hall about 100 times, my mobile phone buzzes in my pocket, caller unknown.

"Hello?"

"Joey, it's me Amy."

"Where the hell are you? You said you would be 20 to 30 minutes that was an hour ago!"

Silence.

I take a deep breath. "Amy, where are you?"

"I'm sorry Joey."

"Listen Amy, are you on your way back? How long will you be?"

"I'm not on my way back."

"What the—what?"

"I'm not on my way back."

"What? How much longer you going to be then?"

"Joey, I'm not coming back."

"Huh?"

"I've tried Joey, I just can't cope. I've tried and I've tried, I need some time Joey, just need some time to get my head straight, so I think Rosie would be better off with you just for a short time."

Oh my God, I feel like I'm falling into a black hole, falling deep into a big black hole.

"Amy you can't do this to me, you just can't dump her on me, just because you're having a bad day."

"Having a bad day, do you think that's all this is? Do you think I want to do this?"

"Look Amy just come back, we can sit down and talk about this." I can hear her sniffing, I think she's crying.

"Joey, do you think I want to leave Rosie? I love her but right now, I'm not coping. I think she would be better off with her dad."

"She's your daughter Amy, she's better off with her mum."

"She's your daughter too."

"But you're its mum."

"And you're her dad," Amy shoots back. "And Joey, what do you think I know about bringing up a kid? I hardly knew my Dad and my mum had to work three jobs to put food on the table and to juggle the bills, she didn't bring me up because she was never there and if she was there, she was exhausted or drunk. I brought myself up and I don't know how to bring anyone else up, I love Rosie too much to ruin her life."

"But Amy, you can't leave it here."

"I have to Joey, if she stays with me, I'm afraid."

"Afraid of what?"

Amy didn't reply.

"Answer me, afraid of what?" I shout.

"Of what I might do, of what might happen," Amy's voice was barely a whisper.

"I don't understand, Amy."

"Joey, I love our daughter. I'd die for her but I have no life, Rosie and I have been living in my aunt's box room in her tiny flat with no chance of getting anything better. I gave up my life, my friends, my dreams for Rosie and sometimes when it's just me and her and she won't stop crying, sometimes the thoughts in my head scare me. Rosie deserves to be with someone who can look after her properly."

"Oh my God. And you think that's me, I don't know the first thing about babies."

"Maybe not but you'll learn, you always have more patience than me. And you've got your Dad and your brother and a big house and your friends."

"Amy, you've got to be joking, don't do this."

"I'm sorry but I'm going now, tell Rosie I love her, tell her every day for me, Joey."

"Amy, no!" but she's gone, she's hung up. Straightaway, I tried to call her back but the number is dead. I stand there just staring at my phone, unable to take in what's happened. I feel my body is shaking.

I keep thinking this is some kind of sick joke but the twisting pain in my stomach and my shaking body tells me otherwise. She's dumped her baby on me and she's free and clear.

And what about me? I've been truly lumbered with a kid which I've been told is mine. Well no, this isn't happening. I'm off to university in less than a month and there's no way that Amy and her baby are going to ruin my plans or my life.

5

Joey

All the time, the baby has been getting louder and louder, my world is out of control, my life is going down the plug hole. NO WAY! I have to do something about that damned noise, I go over to the buggy to take a look down at the thing that's supposed to be my daughter.

How can I have a kid? 10 minutes of not much with Amy and now I've got this thing screaming at me, I can't think straight with all the screaming.

"Can't you stop crying?" How stupid is that asking the thing in the buggy to stop crying. God, the noise is doing my head in. I've got to do something, I push the buggy to the front of the window; perhaps if it can see outside, it might stop. I take out my phone and head for the kitchen, I've called Zoe.

"Zoe, do you remember Amy? Amy Hunter," I launch into her before she has time to even say hello.

"The girl who disappeared after Christmas a while ago?"

"Yeah that's her."

"What about her?"

"You two were friends, Zoe?"

"Well, we weren't best buddies, just kind of knew her in the crowd."

"I don't suppose you have a contact number for her or an address for her aunt?"

"No and why would I? And why would I have Amy's aunt's contact details?"

"Well, Amy went to live with her aunt so I thought you might—"

"How do you know that, Joey?"

"Amy told me."

"When did she tell you?"

Dammit. "Er a while ago."

"Wait a minute, she was your girlfriend back in the day, why are you so keen to get in touch now?"

"No reason," I say feebly, "I was just wondering about her."

"Funny, you start thinking about her now?"

"So do you know anyone that might be in contact with her?"

"Nope sorry not a clue, as far as I know she didn't keep in touch with anyone."

"I'm guessing you got your exam results?" asks Zoe.

"Yeah, four A stars."

"That's brill Joey but I knew you'd walk it, Mr Egghead."

"Thanks. But I'm thinking what am I going to do?"

"Well?" Zoe prompts.

"What?"

"Aren't you going to ask me my exam results?" she asks sounding a bit peeved.

"Yeah of course, I was just about to. Did you get the grades you wanted?"

"Yep, three A stars and an A, so we will be going to the same uni, I can't wait."

"Neither can I," I reply faintly.

Zoe and I applied to the same university more by luck than design. She wants to study computer science. Zoe is determined to have a career that will make her name and her fortune.

Her older sister is a social worker who according to Zoe got paid a whole heap of nothing for doing a totally thankless job.

Me? I wanted to be a journalist ever since mum died. Our first choice of university was over 240 km away, which suited me fine as I longed to leave home and be independent.

"It's going to be great," Zoe enthuses, "you still ready to celebrate tomorrow night? It will be fun to see everyone again before we all scatter to the four corners of the earth."

"Doorbell," I lie. "Got to go, talk later." And I hung up before she could say anything else. I look down at my watch, Dad and Eamon would be back soon. I have an hour or less to try and sort out this mess.

I'm trying to sort out this mess in my head too, I can feel the panic travelling through my body taking root inside me. I open the kitchen door and listen, at least the baby has stopped crying now.

No I'm wrong, it was obviously just taking a breather to get back its energy because it is now crying even louder than before. I shut the kitchen door again.

I spend the next 10 to 15 minutes calling round all of my friends that I thought knew Amy to see if anyone has information about where she might be. But no luck, it seems since she left school she hasn't been in contact with anyone, so after about 20 minutes I have to admit defeat.

Oh I know! Facebook, she'll be on Facebook; maybe I can send her a message on there. But I can't find her on there and I try every variation of the name, middle name, surname and first name but still no luck; I'm well and truly stuffed.

I've got to get out of here, I can't be here. I head for the front door, the sound of the crying baby is all around gripping me and smothering me. I open the front door, every bone in my body is telling me to run, get out of there, escape!

But the baby is still sobbing in the next room. I slam the front door shut and then run up the stairs until I reach my bedroom. I throw myself down on the bed and stare up at the ceiling.

Let me go to sleep, let this be a dream or should I say a nightmare. What am I going to do? I can't just lie here doing nothing. I need to get Amy to come back and take her child away; how do I do that when I can't contact her.

I feel the walls are closing in on me and there's nothing I can do about it. I'm staring up at the ceiling and waiting for inspiration or for Amy to return, for this nightmare to end.

No. Maybe there is an end, my alarm will ring and wake me up. Just for any way out and I wait. After about 10 minutes, the noise downstairs seems to have stopped.

I don't move. I'm waiting, oh God, I hear the key in the door, my Dad and Eamon returning.

6

Joey

I sit up. "Joey, we're back," Eamon shouts from downstairs, "did you get your results? I bet you passed them all."

"Did you pass?" Dad's voice follows Eamon's upstairs.

I go to the top of the stairs and sit on the step. My heart is pounding, Dad and Eamon are staring up at me. "So, how did you do?" Eamon asks again.

"Four A stars."

"I knew it," says Eamon with a big grin on his face.

"So you passed then?" says Dad.

I should be happy but I just feel disappointed but what did I expect? Praise for getting my A-levels, praise for working my butt off. Some hope.

"Yes, I managed to pass."

"Great son, good for you."

Don't strain yourself dad, don't compliment me too much, it's the Irish way. I remember after a football match where I played really well and everyone is complimenting me and I would say to dad.

"I played really well, didn't I?"

His response would always be the same, "don't get fecking big headed, you played okay but you made a lot of errors as well and you were selfish with the ball. Plenty of room for improvement, lad."

And there it was BEING IRISH MEANS YOU'RE NEVER GOOD ENOUGH and being Irish Catholic means we carry an iceberg of guilt.

"You'll be going to university then?" says Dad. I glance towards the sitting room.

"That's the plan."

With that, Dad heads towards the kitchen, saying as he goes, "if I had your chances, I'll be a millionaire," and if I had a pound for every time I heard him say that, I'd be a billionaire by now.

Dad turns and says, "I'm making a coffee, anyone want one?"

"No thanks," we both say at the same time.

"So bro, four A stars means you're off to uni, so can I have your room? Dad, can I paint Joe's room, when he leaves?"

And all the time in the sitting room.

This is unbearable. I don't know what to do or say, I glanced towards the slightly ajar sitting room door. Eamon started up the stairs, grinning away at the prospect of getting my room.

Then an unmistakable sound came from the sitting room. Not as loud as before but audible. Eamon's head whips round towards the direction of the noise.

"What in god's name?" Dad emerges from the kitchen. I stand up, my heart is leaping and my stomach is flipping. Dad heads to the sitting room closely followed by Eamon, I come down the stairs slowly.

"Joey, what's going on? Why is there a baby in here?" I stand there unable to answer, he turned to me and I didn't answer.

"Joey?"

"Its—Amy brought it round. Do you remember her? Amy Hunter. Its name—the baby's name is Rosie."

"Amy is here?" Dad looked up to the ceiling with a frown.

"Ooh! Joey's got a girlfriend and she's upstairs?" says Eamon grinning. At that moment, I just wanted to punch him.

"She's not my girlfriend and she's not upstairs, she's gone."

"Gone where?" asks Dad.

"She said she was going to get nappies and other stuff," I replied, "but she—"

"What?" Dad's frown deepens.

I swallowed hard. "She's not coming back, dad."

"What the hell?" Dad looks at the baby and looks at me and back again. "Why would she leave her little sister here?"

"It's not her sister dad, it's her daughter."

"Her daughter? Why would she—oh sweet Jesus." Dad is staring at me. "Eamon, go upstairs to your room and do something," he snaps, "and shut the door behind you."

"And do, what," replies Eamon.

"Do anything, just feck off," and Dad's glare sweeps back over me like a searchlight, leaving me with nowhere to hide and I'm in no doubt of what he's thinking.

7

Joey

I fall into the armchair. Dad moves back towards the buggy, staring down at its contents. How I wish I could tell what Dad is thinking now. The baby looks up at him just as intently as he is looking at it. Its arms are outstretched.

Dad leans down and takes the now sniffling baby out and holds it close to his chest. The crying stops almost at once and it lays its head on Dad's shoulder. Time passes in hollow heartbeats then Dad turns around and looks at me.

"Joey, what's going on?" Dad asks softly. "Why did she leave her baby here? And what did you mean when you said she's not coming back?"

"Amy said she couldn't cope." I can't look at Dad, so I'm talking to the carpet, almost bent double by the weight on my shoulders.

"Why would she leave her daughter here, Joey? Joey, I ask you a question."

"She said, Amy said, she said it's my daughter, she said I'm the dad."

The terrible silence stretches out and I'm forced to raise my head, I sit up slowly in the chair. I need to know what Dad is thinking no matter how painful it might be. But he's just staring at me, his eyes wide, his mouth open. With some effort he gets it together.

"This is your daughter?" he asks his eyes never leaving my face.

"I don't know."

"But she could be?"

"Yes," I mumbled.

"You stupid bloody eejit," Dad says with intensity, "you stupid fool." His voice is too soft. I wanted him to shout, he's too quiet. Dad closes his eyes and he turns his face away from me, he opens his eyes but he still can't look at me and I find it hard to breathe as I watch him. When he finally looks at me again, his laser gaze pins me to the armchair.

He slowly shakes his head.

Come on Dad, shout at me, call me all the names under the sun, these are the thoughts rattling round in my head.

"How could you be so fecking stupid?" Oh here it comes. I can hear the anger in his voice. "Joey, I never thought I needed to worry about you the way I worry about Eamon because I thought you had common sense, your mum always said you were the sensible one with your head screwed on straight and Eamon was the dreamer."

The way Dad looks at me with such anger in his eyes, makes me feel sick to my stomach. "Do you wanna know something? Your mother would spin in her grave if she knew this, it's the first time ever I'm glad that she isn't around to witness you fucking up your life because that's what you've done." That one cut deep, it found its target more than any other of Dad's other criticisms.

"I don't think you get it, do you?" he says shaking his head, "I wanted you to aspire to something more than having a kid at seventeen, Jesus! Sure you're still a kid yourself but not anymore Joey, now you're a grown-up. For God sake, I thought I brought you up better than this."

I don't want any of this, doesn't Dad realise that? I want to do something with my life, I want to be someone, doesn't he understand that? Dad looked down at the wiggling bundle in his arms, "so the mother has run off and left you holding the baby?"

I nodded.

Dad smiled grimly, "how ironic."

"What d'you mean?"

"Doing a runner is usually the man, not the woman," he walks over to me, "go on, take her."

"What?"

"Take your daughter, Joey."

"No I can't, I might drop her," I'm looking for any excuse not to take her.

"You won't drop her Joey, just hold her like you mean it." I don't move, I can't move, I don't want to hold that thing. But one of us has to give in and I knew it wouldn't be Dad. I took the thing, holding it awkwardly. It wiggles and it's on the verge of crying again.

"Hold her properly, let her feel safe," says Dad.

How the hell do I do that? Terrified of dropping it, I bring it closer to my chest and adjust my grip until its cheek is against my shoulder. Luckily, it settles and stays still. It brings up one tiny hand clenched in a fist to rest against my T-shirt.

It's giving off a baby smell of milk and lotion, its body is warm against mine, its hair is soft and silky under my chin. And I hate it.

Dad sits down on the sofa, "tell me everything that happened this morning."

So I told him—the edited version but even that sounded damning. When I finish, he shakes his head again, he is beyond angry but unlike most people, the angrier he got the quieter he became.

"So were you and Amy regularly sleeping together?"

Oh crap, this is not a conversation I want with my Dad, I can feel my face burning.

"It was only once Dad, just once at a party and we both drank quite a lot."

"Not too drunk to have sex but too drunk to use protection," says Dad.

"It was only once," I mutter.

"Only once, well once was enough, wasn't it Joe? You're holding proof of that in your arms," says Dad, "is there going to be more girls turning up here with babies?"

"No," I say quietly. "I've never had sex with anyone else and only the once with Amy."

And now I'm the colour of a beetroot. Dad is looking at me obviously deciding I'm telling the truth, as his face relaxes slightly and he's not clenching his jaw now.

8

Eamon

I can't believe what I'm hearing, obviously I didn't go upstairs as Dad requested. I'm sitting on the bottom step listening to the procedures. I can't believe our Joey Mr Goody two shoes, Mr Brainbox has made such an error. Joey, a Dad, what next.

And he's only had sex with one person and only had sex once and now has a baby; that's pretty unlucky. Seriously though, I think having a little baby in the house will be lovely. This makes me an uncle, I'm an uncle at age 16, well 17 soon.

I think this might work out well for me though, it will take the limelight away from me as I think Dad is starting to question my sexuality; well to be fair, I'm surprised its taken him this long to work it out. Whereas I've always known. But I think Joey is still in denial.

9

Dad

"I can't believe you had a child and I'm only hearing about it now."

"Dad, I only heard about it today too."

"You didn't know Amy was pregnant?" asks Dad.

I shake my head.

"Why didn't you take the trouble to find out?" I can't answer but my silence is answer enough for Dad.

"I thought Joey that I brought you up well, not dragged you up and we spoke about sex and taking precautions, of being thoughtful and responsible in a relationship but you dump that all out the window for a quick sexual thrill while drunk."

"Dad, it never occurred to me that she might be pregnant."

"I thought you were smart. But now you're saying you don't know how babies are made?" says Dad, "you told me that we didn't need to have the chat about the birds and the bees because it has been covered at school, so was that a lie Joey or did you skip those lessons?"

My whole body is burning up now, I think I might spontaneously combust.

"No, Dad. It was covered at school," I reply.

"Then why Joe, are you holding a baby?"

"I thought Amy might be on the pill or something, as she never told me she was pregnant and then she left school and I didn't see her till today."

"It doesn't matter Joey what you thought or assumed, it takes 2 to make a baby, you should've damn well made sure she couldn't get pregnant by using a FECKING CONDOM." The baby starts to stir because Dad raised his voice, I pulled my face away from its head, trying to make as little contact as possible.

"Joe hold the child properly, she's not a bag of rubbish, she's your daughter."

I took a deep breath and stopped pulling away. Neither I nor Dad are talking as we both try to grasp what's happened.

"Dad, what am I going to do?" I can feel a tear trickle down my cheek, I wipe it away quickly. For the life of me, I can't figure out what to do. I feel trapped, totally stuffed. I start to tremble and I can't make it stop.

"I'm off to uni in a few weeks, so I can't look after a baby." Dad is just staring at me. "Dad?" I say quietly.

He shakes his head. "Joe, you have a daughter now."

"I can't look after it, Dad."

"You've got no choice, son."

"Maybe I could put it up for adoption or to be fostered?" I realise straight away I should've kept my mouth shut, Dad's face looks like thunder.

"You'd give up your own flesh and blood because she's an inconvenience for you?" asks Dad, "and you realise adoption means giving up your own daughter for good, is that what you really want?"

"Yes! I'm seventeen for God sake, of course I don't want to be saddled with a kid at seventeen."

I feel guilty saying it but I couldn't help it. I don't want it, this thing I'm holding is stopping my life from going forward, all my dreams would be squashed, this thing would ruin my life.

"There's no way you can put her up for adoption without the mother's consent and you said you don't know where Amy has gone and it's probably the same with fostering."

"So what's your next bright idea, Einstein? Going to leave the baby on the doorstep somewhere?"

"No way, of course not." I'm shocked, did Dad really think I would do such a thing? His opinion of me must be so low.

"Joe, if your daughter wasn't in the room, I think I might punch you, here you sit thinking only of yourself not of your child or how this is going to affect us all, we're all going to have to live with the consequences of your actions."

"But Dad I can't deal with this, what do I know about babies, I'm only 17, what should I do about that?"

"I really don't think you have many choices Joey," says Dad slowly.

I know what he's thinking. "Dad, I have no money, no job, no way of looking after it and I've only just got my A-level results for fuck's sake! Help me here dad, I didn't plan any of this and I'm not congratulating myself."

"Stop Joey take a breath, breathe and listen to what I'm saying, you have a child, no matter what you do from here forward, if you give her up or keep her, your world has changed and it will never be the same again, nothing you do or say now is going to change the fact that you have a daughter, so you need to get your head straight and accept it just like I'm having to."

"There's nothing I can give her Dad, she is better off without me."

"You can give her the same as I gave you and your brother; a safe place, food on the table and being there for her when it counts."

But I'm hardly listening to him, why isn't he listening to me? I cannot be responsible for anyone else. I'm trying to make a life for myself.

"So can you look after the baby, Dad when I go to university?" Dad starts to laugh not a real laugh, kind of sarcastic laugh.

"I have a full-time job so tell me Joey, how am I going to work and look after your daughter at the same time?"

"Well, how am I supposed to look after a baby and go to uni at the same time?" I say throwing his words back at him.

I look down at the peacefully sleeping baby in my arms. The silence between us speaks volumes. "Well, I'm sure if someone can't cope, it's okay for the child to be taken away and placed with foster parents." I still wasn't willing to give up on that idea.

"So do you want to dump this baby with strangers?"

"I'm a stranger to her," I point out.

"Well Joe, you don't have to be and now you have to make the most important decision of your life."

"What about uni?"

"What about Rosie!" Dad replies angrily.

"I haven't a clue how to look after it."

"Well you will have to learn and quickly, this is what happens when you play growing up games."

"Joe you have a daughter, her name is Rosie and you need to get your act together quickly, you're not walking away from her without even trying to make it work."

"Lots of guys walk away," I point out.

"Well you're not other guys Joe, you are my son and I brought you up better than that, you don't run away, you're not a coward, you face up to your problems."

"So what am I supposed to do?"

"Take a deep breath and man up, you have a daughter that needs you."

"Dad, I know what you want me to do," I snap at him, "but then what? Work in a burger joint or Call Centre, sweep the streets?"

"If that's what it takes," replies Dad, "do you think I work laying cables because I like it, Joey? Do you think it was my dream job? I do it so you and Eamon can achieve your dreams, so that you get a better life than me, that's what a parent does."

"But I'm not a parent! I don't want to be a parent, flipping burgers or laying cables to make a living."

"Well you better get used to the idea Joe because that's what you are, a parent; so man up and stop acting like a spoiled child and if you have to flip burgers or lay cables for a living at least it's honest work, do you not think I had dreams once? We adjust our lives according to circumstances."

"You have a family to support, Joey."

Family? Dad and Eamon are my family, I don't need anyone else, this baby will never belong in my family and would never be wanted by me.

"Joe look at your daughter," says Dad.

"What?"

Dad walks over to me and adjusts my hold on the baby so she is lying in the crook of my arm, its eyes are closed. I can see its face, it's the first time I've really looked at it. Its face is round and it has such long eyelashes, a little pink mouth, how could such a loud noise come out of such a small mouth?

Its hair is black and it frames its face. It's asleep and I can feel the warmth from it, I think it's exhausted from all the crying, I know I feel exhausted. Dad's watching me, I can feel his eyes burning into me.

I think he's expecting me to look at it and think, oh yes I'm going to give up uni and flip burgers for the rest of my life to have this thing in my life that I would look at it and suddenly realised how much I love it? But I feel nothing when I look at it and that scares me, I should surely feel something?

10
Dad

Jesus Christ what a mess, I never thought Joey would bring a baby to our door, not like this anyway. But he doesn't seem to be able to get his head round the fact that he is now a father and has to deal with the situation.

It's like history repeating itself, how I wish I could change all this for him. My heart goes out to him, he looks in total shock, which I suppose he is; it's not every day you get left holding the baby.

How could this Amy just walk away from her baby? I thought mothers were supposed to have a special bond with their child or is that just an old-fashioned thought?

I thought it was Eamon I would have to worry about. I know he's gay but he thinks I don't know and I don't know how to bring up the subject, so I'm waiting for him to announce it and then I can tell him that I don't mind one way or the other.

11

Joey

Dad runs a hand through his hair, "Jesus Christ what a mess," he says more to himself than to me. "Oh Joey," Dad sighs, "you're supposed to be smarter than—"

"Smarter than?"

"Smarter than that Joey, you're supposed to know that actions have consequences, smarter than to end up with a child at seventeen."

So I've proved to him I'm not smart, I just wish you could understand how I feel.

Dad goes to the buggy and take the oversize bag from the buggy handle, he sits on the sofa and starts emptying it. Formula milk, nappies, a baby bottle, a book with chewed corners and envelope stuffed with papers, baby wipes, pink plastic bags (I know what they are for). Baby grow thingy, feeding cup, some jars of baby food.

Dad starts to pull out the papers from the envelope and starts to sift through them.

"What are they?" I ask.

"Medical records from the look of it," he pushes them back into the envelope. "They can wait, I need to think."

What does he need to think about? It's me who is up to my neck in crap. Dad seems to read my mind or perhaps my expression because he answers my unspoken question.

"Priorities, Joe. We need to concentrate now on getting the most important things sorted," there is sadness in his eyes and he gives a sigh. "I wish your mother was here, she was far more practical than me, she would know how to handle this."

"What priorities d'you mean?" I ask.

"Well, Rosie is going to need food and nappies and somewhere to sleep and I'm sure there's a lot more, that's all I can think of right now."

"You mean like a cot?"

"Of course."

"And to put this here, I don't think that's practical."

Dad nodded, "that's why it will be in your room at the foot of your bed."

What are you kidding? "WHAT? No way."

"Where else is she going to go, Joey?"

"I thought maybe in with you?"

"Jeanie Mac Joey! You've got some neck."

Dad glances down at his watch, "I'd better head to the shops. Otherwise they'd be closed before I know it."

"So you're saying it's sleeping in my room?"

"Of course, that way if Rosie needs feeding or changing during the night, you can get up and deal with it, then rock her back to sleep."

"You're kidding, you know I need my eight hours sleep a night uninterrupted."

"Welcome to the world of parenting," he says smiling, he's going towards the door but turns back to face me as he reached it. "Joey?"

"Yes Dad?"

"You can stop calling Rosie 'it' and 'she', use her name and will you be okay for about an hour?"

"No!"

"Joey. Just keep calm. I know this is a shock to you, well it's a shock for all of us, including Rosie. So just don't do anything stupid, you can get through this, we all can, just hang in there, okay? I'll be back soon."

And with that he leaves the room. Then, "JAYUS Eamon, what the feck? So you've been listening at the bloody door?"

"Yes Dad," came the reply from my nosey brother, Eamon loves to know everything about everyone. "Well Dad it's the only way I find out anything in this house by listening at the door."

"I'll be back soon, get in there Eamon and help your brother look after Rosie till I get back."

I stand up to put the baby back in its buggy but as soon as I move, it immediately starts to stir and makes a whimper, so I sit back down quickly as I can't listen to it roaring again. The baby quietened down straight away.

The moment Dad shut the front door, Eamon starts, "Did I hear right?" His eyes as bright as a full moon and his mouth in a big grin. "You've got a daughter?"

I shrugged. I still wasn't going to admit to that, just on Amy's word.

"This is Rosie."

"Whoa." Eamon stares at me with his mouth open, his expression is a confused cocktail of disbelief and astonishment, then he surprises me by saying, "can I hold her?" He comes over to me tiptoeing in case he wakes her.

I rise up from the chair and stretch out my arms to hand it over but then I hesitate.

"Er, you'd better sit down first," I advice.

Eamon sits down, no argument. He stretches out his arms and yet I hesitate.

"I won't drop her," Eamon promised. "Please let me hold her."

I place the baby in his arms. It stirs and kicks out one leg but it doesn't wake up. Eamon readjusts his grip so the baby lays securely in his arms. He kisses its forehead and starts to rock her gently.

"She's so beautiful, Joey," says Eamon, "hello, my little Rosie," he whispers to her, "you are so beautiful. You must take after your mum because you sure didn't get your good looks from your dad."

"I'm your Uncle Eamon, good looks passed your daddy and waited for me to be born."

"She's gorgeous, she smells amazing like kind of fresh," Eamon raises his head and smiles at me but only for a second. He can't tear his gaze away from the baby.

That fries my brain. My little brother, an uncle at sixteen dammit and he's so happy about it, he can't stop smiling at the baby. Then the baby opens its eyes. Oh no, here we go, it's gonna kick off again but it doesn't; it looks up into Eamon's eyes and smiles. Then it closes its eyes and goes straight back to sleep.

"I'm your Uncle Eamon and I love you so much." Eamon kisses Rosie once again on the top of the head. Rosie has smiled at him and I've never heard Eamon say he loves anyone but just like that he loves the baby. How does that work and why do I feel so empty?

12

Eamon

Joey is so lucky, he has his own little special person now. But Joey doesn't seem to want her. I'm hoping it's just shock and he will recover. Poor Rosie, her mum doesn't want her and Joey's made his feelings on Rosie pretty clear.

She should have been born into a loving little family but I love her and Dad loves her; I can tell and I think Joey will in time, she's beautiful.

It's funny. I feel an instant connection with little Rosie. I would love to have children but I'm destined to be a gay uncle. I'm surprised Dad has taken it so well, I mean I know he's as mad as a March hare but he's being practical and getting stuff done.

I wonder if Joey's present girlfriend Zoe knows that Joey's ex Amy has left him holding the baby. Oh to be a fly on the wall in that conversation, Zoe is a selfish bitch anyway. I can't stand her but I get a feeling that it's mutual.

It's funny that I and Joey have always known what we wanted to do in the future, Joey dreams of becoming a journalist and me a singer song writer.

But it looks to me that Joey's dream might not make reality.

Tonight, I was going to sit down with both of them and tell them I'm gay but I think they have had a big enough shock today, so I'll leave it for another time.

13

Joey

Eamon is happy to continue holding the baby, which is fine by me. I've got things to do, like trying to find a way out of this predicament. I dash upstairs and go on the internet and look up fostering and adoption and paternity tests.

It seems Dad was right about the adoption, it would be bloody difficult without Amy's agreement. And the information I found that fostering seems to be more difficult than adoption. All sorts of social workers, health workers have to get involved apparently.

Just more people to witness the mess I've made of my life. Every page I scanned about fostering made me feel more and more disgusting. This was supposed to be my daughter and here I am searching for ways to get rid of it.

But I wasn't thinking of myself, I swear I wasn't, I mean, what do I have to offer a baby? In spite of what Dad said, it'd be far better off without me. I need to establish once and for all if this baby is mine.

That meant a DNA test. So I googled DNA test not expecting much. To my surprise, there are loads of online organisations to carry out DNA tests, to establish paternity. I studied the details.

It looks straightforward enough, if I cough up my hard earned money, then they would send me a DNA test kit and all I have to do was swap the inside of my mouth or cheek cells with a cotton bud and I have to do the same to the baby, then send off the swabs.

Five days after that they would send me the results and then I would know once and for all whether or not I was the baby's father. It's not that I didn't believe Amy but she might have made a mistake.

I mean she must've made a mistake in spite of what she said. I just got to know for sure. Nothing else could happen till I knew for sure. I found the number provided by one site which seems more professional than the others.

I'll try to make myself sound more mature and I give the woman at the other end, my details and the number of my one and only debit card. The fee is more than half of all the money I have in the world but I figure that if the outcome was the one I wanted, it would be a small price to pay.

I head back downstairs and Eamon is exactly where I left him, as soon as I come into the room, he smiled at me whispering, "she's still asleep."

Dad already has a plan of action which he is following up and Eamon and Dad are so accepting. They are both swimming, I am the only one drowning. I flop down in a chair opposite Eamon and watch how he holds the baby so naturally like it was no big deal, like he's been doing it for years.

"She's lovely," Eamon said softly, "you're so lucky."

"Lucky? Are you kidding?"

"Well, you get to be loved unconditionally; well, at least until Rosie realises you are a major idiot, probably happen when she's a teenager. That's when most kids realise their parents are cracked."

"Oh yeah, you seem to know a lot about it for a half pint 16-year-old."

"I may be shorter, thinner and younger than you but in everything else, I am greater."

I laughed and it feels good but strange, this day has already lasted forever.

"Modest as ever Eamon," I say.

But the thing is he was right. Eamon is one of those lucky kids who breezes through exams with the minimum of effort not having to study, actually it wasn't just exams but life in general; me on the other hand, slogged my guts out. Funny, smart and good-looking, everything came so easy to him.

"One day, I'm going to be a famous singer songwriter," Eamon has been telling Dad and me this since he was about 10. He wants this more than anything else in the world. He started writing songs from the age of 11 and Dad reckoned he used to sing along in his own way to tunes when he was a baby in his bouncy chair.

Not sure if I believe that one or not. Dad has told him not to set his heart on being a singer. As there's a high chance you won't hit the big time and end up singing in pubs.

Eamon had drawn himself up to face Dad directly and looked him in the eye and said, "they said going to the moon was impossible or inventing penicillin but it was still done. Unlikely things happen every day and if I want it enough, I'll get it in spite of what you think."

"You should have a backup plan in case it doesn't happen," Dad warned when it became apparent that Eamon was actually serious.

Eamon shook his head, "a backup plan means somewhere in my head, I think I might fail and that word is not in my vocabulary, plus I'm too talented to fail."

Dad and I exchange a look and I say to Eamon, "the ego has landed." Which makes both Dad and Eamon laugh.

My brother Eamon.

He grins at me now, then turns back to look at Rosie. "D'you want to hold her for a while?"

"Nah, you're okay, you're doing a fine job," I reply.

Eamon looks at me and he seems sad

"What's the matter, mate?" I ask.

"I'd like to have children one day," says Eamon, "but it's not going to happen."

"You don't know that, when you meet the right girl, you may end up with a football team."

Eamon looks at me. "Do I look like the type of guy who's going to settle down with a good woman?"

"Stranger things have happened, Eamon." I shrug.

"When I settle down, there won't be with a good woman and what's more—"

"Fine," I interrupt. "Go for a bad woman then. They're supposed to be more fun anyway."

"It wouldn't be with a woman at all," Eamon begins.

"Eamon, I don't want to talk about this now."

"No that's it, isn't it?" Eamon says, "you never do, you can't handle the fact that I might be gay."

"Maybe it's a phase you're going through and you'll grow out of it."

"Did you go through this phase?" asks Eamon.

"Well no I didn't but I did read somewhere some boys do."

"Okay. So when are you going to grow out of your phase?"

"Huh?"

"This heterosexual phase you're going through?"

"Shut the fuck up, Eamon."

"I'm just asking," says Eamon, "you know what? When you grow out of yours, I'll grow out of mine."

"Look Eamon, I just don't want you to get hurt, you need to be—dammit, you're my little bro."

"I need to be what Joey. In the closet?"

"That's not what I meant. I just don't want you to get hurt."

Eamon gives me a smile, "I know Joey but it's my life, my mistakes to make."

"Damn it Eamon, you're fucking hard work."

"Stop swearing in front of your daughter," says Eamon. "Did you love Amy?" asks Eamon unexpectedly.

I don't need to think about this as I shake my head.

"That's a pity," says Eamon.

"Why?"

"Someone as special as this little one should've been made with love."

"She shouldn't have been made at all!"

"Well, she's here now Joey and she's not going anywhere."

"I don't know about that Eamon," I reply.

"D'you think Amy will come back for her?"

"Please yes, sweet Jesus," I reply. We both sit in silence, both staring at Rosie, she looks so small and helpless, my daughter Rosie. I close my eyes, I feel like crying, I wait and open them as I pull myself together, only to see Eamon kissing

Rosie on the forehead again, how I wish I was more like my brother.

His view on life is so different than mine, his mind-set is to trust everyone and accept everything until he has reason not to. That attitude worries me. He's so naive and innocent. He makes me feel like the most cynical bastard ever.

14

Joey

When the old fella finally returned home, it took me and him three trips to the car to bring in all the stuff he just bought. I swear he spent a fortune, looks like he's cleared out the baby store; everything now is in the living room, it looks like an obstacle course of boxes.

There was a ready to assemble cot and enough disposable nappies to soak up all the water in the Irish Sea. A baby carrier thingy that lets you carry a baby against your chest so your arms are free, a bottle of baby bath, baby moisturiser, baby cream for nappy rash and if you have a pharmaceutical item you can think of to go with a baby, we've got it.

Cutlery baby bottles, a bottle steriliser, baby bedding, a highchair, a few toys; a teddy bear and a doll, a ball and a couple of picture books, dresses, more little baby clothes, booties, little suede Ugg style boots with soft soles, baby wipes, baby baby baby baby.

Rosie is now waking and Eamon hands her back to me. Eamon is running around like a child looking at everything, like a child at Christmas. I look at Rosie, how it could be possible such a small person needs so much stuff. That's when it hits me how clueless I really am.

"This lot must've cost a fortune," I say, shocked by the amount the old fella has bought.

"They're for my granddaughter, okay?" says Dad, "everything else after this is down to you, Joey."

Down to me? I'll be broke in a week and what's more worrying Dad has bought the stuff like he thinks Rosie is staying for a while whereas I'm thinking a day or two; maybe a week at the very longest just until I get back the results of the DNA test.

Rosie is wiggling in my arms, reaching out with both arms for the stuff on the carpet. From the strange noise she is making, it seems she's just as excited as Eamon.

"Put her down," says Dad, "she just wants to explore."

"Is it safe?"

Dad smiles at me. "Yeah, just be ready to pick her up if it looks like she's about to touch something that she shouldn't."

Frowning, I place the baby on one of the few bare patches of carpet. Rosie takes off like a shot. I've never seen anyone move that fast on all fours! We all burst out laughing and then look at each other in surprise.

I can't remember the last time we all shared a laugh, I couldn't understand myself as I was about as far from being in a laughing mood as it was possible to get.

Rosie crawls over to the sofa then tries to pull herself up. She lands on the bottom three times but she doesn't cry or protest, she just keeps trying, finally she manages to stand wobbling a bit but staying upright.

"Jaysus Dad, she can walk?" I say in amazement.

"Not yet, she can stand though, so walking isn't too far away," says Dad.

Rosie bypasses the teddy and goes for the baby wipes, she pulls them towards herself and then sits down with a thump, taking the wipes with her. And she is examining the package like it's truly riveting.

Moments pass as we all stand watching. After a few moments, Dad says, "right, first things first we need to sort out the cot."

"Eamon you're with me, you can help me put the cot together while Joey looks after Rosie."

"Not me, Dad," says Eamon, "these are the hands of a musician not a manual labourer."

"Kop yourself on Eamon, I can't do it on my own," Dad frowns.

"Fine then, I'll look after Rosie and Joey can help you with the lifting and shifting."

Dad sighs, "Eamon, Joey needs to spend time with his daughter, they've got to get to know each other and Joey has to get used to being with her."

"That's not fair," Eamon complains.

"Suck it up, buttercup," says Dad, quoting one of Eamon's favourite quotes back to him. "Now move your backside and help me carry this cot upstairs."

I envy Eamon. I'd rather be assembling the cot then looking after the baby. My mind drifts back to this morning and all I had to worry about was my A-level results and now I've got all this to deal with, this can't be happening.

"Joey, wake up! You stay down here, keep an eye on Rosie and sort all the stuff out."

"D'you really think she's mine?" The words are out of my mouth before I can stop them. Eamon and Dad both turn and look at me. "Never mind," I mumble.

"Of course she's yours, she looks just like you," says Eamon.

"I thought all babies are supposed to look like Winston Churchill," I say, eyeing Rosie doubtfully.

Dad laughs, "yeah, they look like Churchill for about a day after they're born; after that, they take on their own looks and personalities and Eamon is right, she looks just like you."

Eamon bends down and places the tips of his fingers under the cot box. "I bet this gives me blisters," he moans as he starts to lift it.

Dad rolls his eyes. "This is going to be painful alright," he sighs and winks at me.

15

Eamon

Well that was deeply unpleasant. I've never done anything like that and I'm never again doing anything like that. I'll pay someone if I need anything in the future. Still it was for a good cause, for my lovely little niece.

I still can't get my head round saying that. My niece. I do like the sound of it though even if it is a little strange. But it must be even stranger for Joey I bet. 'Daughter' will sound really weird to my brother.

Poor Joey, he looks like he's going to puke his guts up at any second, he looks like a rabbit caught in the headlights. And Dad being all efficient hoping Joey will follow his lead and get on with things as he obviously can't get out of the situation.

But I don't think Joey sees it that way. I can understand that as I still can't get over it. Joey—Mr Boffin, Mr Truth, justice and the Brophy way, I mean every second of his life he has planned for the next 10 years but he now has a kid. A beautiful baby girl.

Study freak by day, stud by night. Ha ha! Wait till I tease him with that one. I wonder how many girls Mr Playboy has slept with. God help us if more women come knocking at the door claiming he's a daddy.

I don't think the old fella will be able to handle it. Time to get out of the shower before I turn into a prune. But at least the shower makes me feel a bit better.

16

Joey

Dad comes downstairs after about 30 minutes with a face like thunder.

"What's up?"

"Your fecking brother that's what's up, he never stopped moaning from start to finish, he's giving me a bloody headache."

"Where is he now?"

"He's in the shower, apparently all that work made him dirty."

Dad sits down in the armchair and looks at Rosie. "Have you picked her up since I've been upstairs?"

I shake my head, "she's been happy playing with her toys."

"Have you spoken to her?"

"To say what?"

Dad sighed. "Joey for god's sake, you need to talk to her all the time, that's how she learn to talk."

"What should I say?"

"For God sake Joey. Anything, everything, that's how she will learn and the two of you will bond, I don't understand you, stop acting stupid and realise this is your daughter. I know it's a big shock for you but now you have to stand up and take responsibility for your actions."

"Dad I'm not stupid but do you think I'm happy about this?"

"Look Joey. I know sometimes I come down on you a bit hard but you've got to stop thinking everything I say to you is a criticism and I know you're not happy with the situation but we're here now, so we all got to get on with it."

"Sometimes a bit harder on me?" I scoff, "I can't remember the last time you praised me for anything, in fact when was the last time you said 'well done Joey'? Hell, when was the first time?"

"And what exactly should I be praising you for? Knocking up some girl and having a baby at seventeen?"

"No Dad, now you're just taking the mick, of course I wouldn't have been praised for that," I reply angrily. "Once in a while, a word of encouragement would be nice."

"I praise you Joey when you do something that deserves it."

"What, so 4 A stars for my A-levels didn't cut it with you?"

"Of course it's good enough, you did well," says Dad.

"Oh my God! Don't put yourself out," I reply.

"I mean it, you've got good results, I knew you would and I'm happy for you."

"Let's be honest that nothing I say or do will ever be good enough for you, will it?"

"Now you're talking rubbish," Dad dismisses.

"Am I? As far as you're concerned, you think of me as a waste of space and this baby just confirms that for you."

61

"That's not true but I had such high hopes for you, I wanted you to be someone, to do something with your life."

"Instead of what I am—I totally screw up with a kid? Well, I'm sorry Dad. SORRY SORRY SORRY."

"Stop shouting at me Joey."

Rosie starts bawling. Not just crying but screaming the house down.

"Rosie has the right idea, the way you two are shouting at each other would make anyone cry," Eamon says from the doorway, "what the hell is wrong with you two shouting like that with the little one in the room."

Dad stands up, Eamon heads over towards Rosie but I get there first and pick her up.

"Okay Rosie," I whisper. "I'm sorry, it's okay." I hold her close to my body, my hands moving slowly stroking her back, whispering words of apology into her ear. I turn to see Dad and Eamon standing close behind me.

"D'you want me to take her?" asks Dad.

And prove to Dad that I'm a failure in this as well as the rest of my life. I shake my head. "I don't need your help, I can manage."

Rosie keeps moving her head, straining to look over my shoulder; it takes a few seconds but I finally realise why. "Rosie, your mum isn't here, she's gone away and left you with me. She's not here and she's not coming back."

"Joey, don't tell the child that," says Dad.

"Why not, it's the truth, isn't it?" I say. "Rosie, you and I are in the same boat up the creek without a paddle."

I don't know if Rosie understands me, probably not but she quiets down and rests her head on my shoulder. I am here, her mum isn't. And at least for this moment, as far as Rosie is concerned, I've done something right.

17
Joey

I can't sleep tonight. Rosie didn't keep me awake, to my surprise she slept the whole night through, so that was an unexpected result.

What keeps me awake is something else, fear. Fear of the unknown. I've never felt fear like this before. More than once I've got up, I have stood at the side of the cot, looking down at Rosie, I find myself stroking her cheek or her hair before I realise what I am doing.

But the more I look at Rosie, the more scared I get but not for me, for her. She deserves better than me. She deserves more than to be dumped by her mum. Quite frankly, she deserves better. But I guess none of us get to choose our parents.

When I look back, it's been a strange evening after Dad and I had our bust up. Usually when me and Dad argue, I usually go up to my bedroom, Dad retreats into his room and Eamon would stay downstairs watching TV alone.

But not this time.

This evening, Dad is assembling the highchair, while Eamon gets down on his knees and starts pulling silly faces at Rosie, making her giggle. I try to make myself useful sorting through all the things that Dad bought. When Dad left the room to take the highchair into the kitchen, Eamon rounds on me.

"What the hell, Joey? What is wrong with you?" he asks lowering his voice after glancing at Rosie.

"Huh?"

"Dad is doing his best and frankly, I can't believe he's handled it so well, so can't you at least meet him halfway?"

"Now wait a minute," I begin, a little cry from Rosie and a scrunched up look of anxiety on her face forces me to smile and change my tone as well. I took a deep breath.

"I'm more than willing to meet halfway but he won't take a step in my direction," I speak softly so I won't upset Rosie. "Did you hear him say congratulations or well done when I told him my exam results? Because I didn't."

"No, I didn't hear that," my brother admits, adopting the same singsong sickly tone for Rosie's benefit, "but I also didn't hear a single thank you from you when you saw what Dad bought for Rosie."

"I did say thanks."

"No, you didn't," Eamon insists. He then turns back to Rosie and starts pulling more faces. Then he picks her up and puts her on her feet. "Go on Rosie, walk to your daddy, go ahead walk to your daddy."

The word daddy makes me feel sick to my core. Dad comes back into the room. "You don't wanna walk to your daddy, Rosie? I don't blame you," says Eamon, thinking he's being funny. "Walk to Grandad instead, can you say Grandad?"

"Jesus, Mary and Joseph!" Dad exclaims. "Grandad? I'm not even 40 yet."

That made it sound like at 38, he was miles away from 40.

As the evening wears on, Eamon doesn't let up. I swear he didn't stop for breath. Dad and I were the total opposite. We didn't say one word to each other. Dad and I moved all Rosie's new things upstairs to my room and the kitchen as necessary with barely a word spoken between us. I kept sneaking glances at him.

Dad.

Funny how before this morning the word meant just the person who is always there for you. Kind of like in the background but you know that if you needed him, he will be there for you in a heartbeat.

The living room was mostly clear of Rosie stuff, just a couple of toys and one or two of the new books was left downstairs for her. We all stay downstairs. I don't know why Dad and Eamon have stayed up but I am relieved as I was more than nervous about being alone with a baby.

Dad turns on the TV, onto some Quiz Show; he wasn't really watching it, his eyes were permanently on Rosie. Eamon was sitting on the carpet and chatting away to Rosie about all her new toys and anything else that popped into his head.

I was sitting in the armchair and just watching. The atmosphere only changes when Rosie starts to grizzle, which quickly turns into something more meaningful.

"You need to feed her, give her a bath and get her ready for bed," Dad informs me.

What I really feel like doing wasn't any of the above. I feel like letting off some steam but that isn't on the menu. Dad nuked a bottle for her and I gave Rosie her first bath with me and I found it nerve racking.

I got just as wet as Rosie with all this messing about she did and I couldn't take my eyes off her for a single second as I had visions of her slipping down into the water. By the time she had her pyjamas on and was in her cot, I was absolutely knackered.

It wasn't just all the physical stuff of food and bath, nappy changes and trying to coax her into lying down and getting some sleep.

It was the mental exhaustion of having to concentrate and pay attention every second.

I can't believe people do this because they want to. Trying to get her to go to sleep was the most exhausting. Every time I lay her down, she would stand by pulling herself up by hanging onto the side of the cot. After the third or fourth time into this, she starts to cry again.

Dad comes into my room as he hears Rosie crying.

"She's in a strange room and she's not used to you yet," says Dad.

"So what should I do?"

"Sit her on your lap and sing to her," Dad suggests.

"Sing?"

Dad smiles, "I suppose you don't remember me singing you to sleep and your mum as well."

"I remember you singing to Eamon but not me."

"Well, we sang to both of you."

"But your singing sucks."

Dad looks at me with one eyebrow raised. "You seemed to like it when you were a baby, especially if your mother sang to you."

Eamon comes into my room as well saying, "I think I remember."

"Do either of you remember what song you always wanted your mum or me to sing?"

I haven't a clue but Eamon pipes up. "I know! I know!" And he starts singing.

"Good morning Fox! Good morning sir

Pray what is that you're eating?

I find fat goose I stole from you

And will you come and taste it?"

Eamon stops but Dad continues the song in Gaelic, his native tongue.

"An maidrin rua rua rua rua

An maidrin rua ata' granna

An maidrin rua ina lu'isa luachair

Is barra Doha' chluais in aired."

Actually, Dad and Eamon singing is pretty good.

"If I were you, I'd make the most of Rosie at this stage, before you know it she'll be looking at you like you're some old eejit who knows nothing about life."

"Is that how I treat you?"

"Most of the time—yeah," says Dad, "but that's what happens when your kids grow older. At least Eamon still thinks there's a tiny bit of life in this old dog yet!"

Dad and I regard each other.

I turn away, "I'll read to her. I think she's upset enough without having to listen to me sing." Picking her up, I go over to my bed and sit down, carefully placing Rosie on my lap, her back to my chest.

I grab one of her bedtime books from the foot of my bed, I have the book in front of both of us and open it but it was damned awkward.

"If you lean her in against your arm, then you'll both be more comfortable and she'll probably fall asleep faster," advised Dad. Which I had to admit worked far better. I read the picture book through twice, explaining the pictures as I went; when I looked Rosie was finally asleep.

Then I moved like an arthritic tortoise to carry her to her cot, praying every second that she wouldn't wake up. And amazingly managed to lie her down without waking her, after supporting her head the way Dad told me. The day was finally over. But mine wasn't.

Everyone in the house is asleep except me; sleep isn't coming to me, I switch on my computer, let the light from the monitor wash over me. Couple of minutes and I'm on my desired page.

I sit there just staring at the screen. I don't know how long for dammit, I had to do this. I couldn't give up my future I just couldn't. I confirm that I will be taking up my place at the university. Now I just have to make sure it happens.

Switching off the computer, I tiptoe back to my bed. I fall asleep thinking everything will be back to normal in the morning; this has just been a nightmare and I'll wake up and everything will be okay.

18
Joey

I wake up to what sounds like a cat meowing or something. I close my eyes again, then I remember. When I manage to make my eyes open, Rosie is standing up holding onto the side of her cot watching me.

I throw my duvet off and jump out of bed. The closer I get to her, the more the smell hits me. And the smell is appalling. I mean really bad, throat catching, nose blistering bad. Don't didn't need to be a rocket scientist to know I am about to be deep in baby poo.

Fuck this, I didn't sign up for this.

There has to be some way out of this, I wasn't going to get stuck with a kid that might not even be mine. Kids are truly mingling, smelly and relentlessly demanding. I don't need that, my life is already full.

There is no room for Rosie. I wasn't going to play this game, putting my life on hold for the next 18 years. No way but for now, I'll do what I have to do just for now.

10 minutes later and the assault on most of my senses is over, Rosie is still grizzling.

"What's wrong now?" I ask, irritation more than evident in my voice. I've changed her nappy, cleaned her and she isn't tired as she has only just woken up, so what is the problem?

She must be hungry, I realise. Reluctantly picking her up, I head downstairs. Dad is already dressed and sitting at the kitchen table with Eamon.

"Hiya Rosie," grins Eamon.

"Morning Angel," says Dad. I'm sure as hell guessing he's not talking to me.

"And good morning to you guys too!"

"I've made some porridge," Dad tells me, "yours is in the microwave. Rosie's baby porridge is on the hob, cooling."

I sit Rosie in her highchair. "I'm not hungry. Could you do it please? I'm going back to bed," I say to Dad.

"What? Where you go, she goes," says Dad, "you don't get to palm her off whenever you feel like it."

Dad and I exchange the look of mutual antagonism. But I could read his expression like one of Rosie's picture books. If I go back to my room, he will make sure Rosie joins me about five seconds later.

With a sigh, I pull her porridge into one of the bowls Dad has bought her. I've got out the matching spoon. I try a spoonful to check the temperature but then I really wish I hadn't. It was bland to the point of being totally tasteless.

"What's up with it?" asks Dad.

"It tastes of nothing."

"It's probably salt free, children of Rosie's age can't handle a lot of salt," Dad tells me.

My bowl of porridge is in the microwave and it's just really hit me; I am hungry, actually I'm starving. I was ready to douse it in maple syrup. Putting Rosie's porridge on her highchair, I hand her the plastic spoon and head to the microwave to get my breakfast.

"Watch out!" Dad yells.

I turn and immediately make an intercepting dive that a premiership goalie would be proud of. Of course it doesn't work, Rosie's porridge hits the floor, followed a second later by her bowl. The spoon is then dropped on my head.

Total silence for a moment, then the room erupts and Rosie bursts out crying.

"Joey, that's what happens when you take your eye off the ball," Dad tells me when he has managed to control himself from laughing. Grabbing some kitchen towels, I start to clean up the mess on the floor.

Dad gets up and puts another helping of baby porridge and milk into the saucepan on the hob. Eamon takes Rosie out of the highchair and starts rocking her.

And all I could think of was, what's going to happen when I have to do this on my own. Suppose I had to clean up the mess and make more porridge and pacify Rosie with no help, all by myself? Is this what Amy had to cope with all alone, day in day out?

"It's okay sweetie, it's okay," Eamon soothes.

"Here, give it to me?" asks Dad opening his arms.

"No it's okay, I've got her," says Eamon.

Dad's hands drop reluctantly to his sides. There it was again, that feeling in the pit of my stomach as I look at them all. I straighten up slowly. Half the porridge must be still on the floor but I don't care.

What did they think they were doing? Eating breakfast, chatting, carrying on like nothing was different. I think I've fallen down a rabbit hole.

"Why are you both acting like this?" I ask.

"Like what?" They both say together.

"Like she's normal," I point to Rosie, "like you're having that here is the most normal thing in the world."

"Joey shut your mouth, you really can be vile!" says Eamon.

"Joey!" Dad glares at me.

"What? I didn't care what they thought, can you tell me then what this is? I'm supposed to be happy that a baby's been dumped on me, the life I want is being flushed down the toilet and you two are acting like it's no big deal, well guess what? It is a big fucking deal."

"Oh yeah, poor Joey. What about poor Rosie?" sniffs Eamon.

I went for him. Dad jumps in between us. "Joey just calm down," he warns me.

"Dad, this is total crap. I'm supposed to believe you think this is normal?"

"Go on then Joey, you tell us how we should behave?" Dad asks. "What do you expect us to do? Scream, throw things, punch all the kitchen doors. Come on what?"

"SHE DOESN'T BELONG HERE!" I shout.

"She belongs with you," says Dad quietly.

"THIS IS YOUR PROBLEM, YOU NEVER LISTEN TO ME, IT'S EITHER YOUR WAY OR THE HIGHWAY!" I shout at him.

Rosie is really crying now, her bottom lip is quivering and she's looking at me like she is scared of me. It was that look from Rosie that got to me. Dad and I might not get on, we have disagreements but I have never looked at him the way she is looking at me.

73

I take a deep breath and said, "don't worry Rosie, I'll clean up this mess and Grandad will make you some more breakfast." Rosie visibly relaxes as I talk to her in that silly singsong voice.

"Nothing like being called Grandad to make you feel old," says Dad winking at me.

It's on the tip of my tongue to say, well you chose to be a grandad but I didn't, I kept quiet.

The anger inside me starts to fizzle out. Now it's just whispering around my body. I've just got to hang in here for a few days and hopefully, I will have my life back. I'm sure I can hang on for a few more days.

I start cleaning up the rest of the mess on the floor but I'm also watching Dad making Rosie's baby porridge. When I make porridge, I just nuke it in the microwave, the baby version seems more involved. Then I see Dad adding goat's milk.

"Why have you bought goats milk?" I ask.

Before Dad could answer, in jumps Eamon. "Babies find it easier to digest than cow's milk," answers Eamon.

"How do you know that?" I ask.

"I looked it up last night just in case you get run over and I have to take over," he says smiling.

I shake my head saying, "Eamon you are just weird."

TAKE TWO.

This time Rosie's breakfast goes okay. After testing the temperature myself, I fed her spoonful after spoonful. She seems to be enjoying it at any rate. But as I'm feeding her, my mind keeps drifting about the day ahead of me and the fear returns to my stomach.

"Dad, are you working today?" I ask.

"Well, I was supposed to but I called in and booked the day off but I'm meeting a few of the guys tonight in the pub," Dad replies.

Relief sweeps over me, I don't want to be alone with the baby, I wouldn't be able to cope. I wouldn't know what to do with her all day. Plus, I am supposed to go out with my mates for a drink later, how is that going to work?

"What about you Eamon, what are you doing today?" asks Dad.

"I'm going shopping with Lucy," Eamon replies.

"For Christ sake, what are you getting now?" Dad asks.

"Just school stuff, Dad," Eamon replies like butter wouldn't melt.

"Oh yeah, sure," replies Dad, "Now don't go spending money I haven't got."

"As if I would."

Dad looks at me and must've seen the look on my face, he says, "I can help you with Rosie today. Okay?"

"Thanks Dad, I appreciate it."

"Hmmm," says Dad with ill grace. But I don't care. All I care about is the fact he wasn't leaving me alone with it. "But I am going out tonight, I'm not missing it as it's a leaving do for John," Dad warns, "and you'll be okay. Rosie will be asleep for the night by the time I leave and I'll only be gone a couple of hours okay?"

"That's great dad, thank you." I would settle for any help I could get. The rest of the day is uneventful. I had to change Rosie's clothes as her PJs were covered in porridge. Then Dad helped me set up a routine for the baby and myself; get it up, change nappy, breakfast, change out of PJ's, playtime, nap, nappy change, lunch, playtime, nappy change, dinner, playtime, bath, nappy change, bed.

"We managed with you and your brother," Dad tells me, "I set up a schedule so we knew what we should be doing at any hour of the day."

It sounds a bit regimental to me but whatever works. And at least I know where I am with a timetable. Luca and a number of my other friends phoned throughout the day to ask about my exam results and chat about the forthcoming party.

Much as I wanted to chat, I couldn't, I had to look after Rosie. But I promised each one that phoned that I'd see them later. The party was my oasis, a glimmer of normality that I so desperately needed.

Rosie seems to be getting used to my face because she no longer wears that look of unease when I pick her up. The day seems to fly by and before I know, it is evening and Dad is ready to go out the door to meet his friends.

"Are you sure you'll be okay?" he asks.

I nod. "Yeah I'll be fine, enjoy yourself."

"Well, Rosie is bathed and ready for bed, so all you have to do is read to her until she's sleepy then put her in the cot and I'll be back before you know it. But if you need me phone me. Okay?"

"Dad, I'll be fine," I insist.

A few seconds after the front door closes, I head back into the sitting room. Eamon is rolling Rosie's ball to her, much to her delight. "Eamon, can you watch Rosie for me? I need to get changed."

"For what?" Eamon frowns.

"The end of school party at the lemon tree," I remind him, "it starts in less than an hour."

76

"Well, tell Luca and all the others you can't make it."

"Are you crazy?" I say aghast. "This will be my last chance to see half of them. And it's going to be a great night, I'm not missing this for anyone or anything."

I glance at an oblivious Rosie, who is sitting on the carpet now playing with assorted toy farm animals my Dad has bought her.

"What about Rosie?"

"What about her?"

"You're going to leave her here alone?" Eamon was scandalised.

"Of course not, you're here, can't you babysit for me?"

"Me? Sorry. No. I'm meeting my friends at the lemon tree too in," Eamon glances down at his watch, exclaiming "in 40 minutes! I need to go and get ready." He jumps to his feet.

"Hang on," I have to grab him and pull him back as he was nearly out of the room.

"Alright, I'll pay you."

Eamon shook his head. "I'm going out, I'm not the one with the kid and no life now."

I have to stop myself from smacking him one. But I try another tact, "Eamon, she's your niece," I say. I don't want him to know how much his words hurt me.

"She's your daughter," Eamon points out, "I think a Dad beats an uncle."

"Oh, come on. You can meet your friends at any time." I wasn't going to give up, "but mine is the end of an era once-in-a-lifetime thing."

"Joey, I'm not changing my plans."

"Not even for your niece?"

Eamon smiles down at Rosie. "Nice try, it's not happening, see you when I get back."

But if he or Dad or anyone else thinks I am going to stay home, then they are dead wrong; no way am I staying in tonight. Rosie will just have to come with me.

19

Joey

I am having second thoughts as I stand outside the lemon tree. I've eaten at the wine bar a number of times and it has a great lively atmosphere but now I think about it, I haven't really seen any young kids or babies in there.

Rosie is asleep in her baby carrier, her face turned sideways against my chest but I can't guarantee she will stay that way once I go inside. It is only 7:30 but looking through the windows, I think the place is already more than a half full. I can't see Eamon though, which was maybe just as well. Hopefully, he won't be able to spot me either. A quick hello to my friends, maybe one drink and then I'll leave.

Checking that Rosie is still asleep, I step inside. The smell of beer, perfume, aftershave and the aroma of cooked food hit me first, quickly followed by laughter, chatter and some kind of music. Glasses clinking, every sound seems amplified.

The trouble was getting into the restaurant area with walking through the noisy bar. I look down at Rosie anxiously but she is still asleep. I'm sad to say I'm not sure how long that will last for.

"Joey! We're over here," Zoe's voice rings out over the general noise. Turning, I see her standing up and beckoning to me. Luca, Max and seven or eight other guys I know and a few girls have already taken over one corner of the restaurant.

They are sitting at a long table which is already covered in drinks and snacks. Zoe is looking as good as always, she wore a bright neon orange T-shirt and black jeans. Jet black hair is tied back in a ponytail and her teardrop earrings glint against her tanned skin, she looks amazing.

My mate Luca is sitting next to her as usual and he is holding a bottle of lager like it is a long lost friend and from the glazed happy look in his dark blue eyes, it isn't his first. I look down at Rosie again, how am I going to explain her?

My decision to bring her with me is beginning to seem like a bad idea. This could turn out to be complicated. I head over towards Zoe and the others.

"Hiya mate," Luca grins as I approach.

"Hey," I smile.

"What the fuck?" Luca isn't the only one to look shocked and stare or do a double take when they realise what I am carrying.

"So how is everyone?" I ask like there isn't a thing wrong. Luca shuffles over so I could sit between him and Zoe. "Hiya, Zoe." I smile, leaning forward.

She tries to meet me at the other end of the offered kiss but the baby gets in the way.

"What's that?" Luca points to the contents of the baby carrier strapped round my upper body.

"What does it look like? A potato?"

"You brought a baby along?" asks Max.

Max is built like an athlete, he is always at the gym and he runs at least 10 KM every day before school and is super fit and healthy but he makes sure everybody knows it. Questions flew at me!

"Are you supposed to be babysitting?"

"Did you get lumbered?"

"You've brought a kid here?"

"Is it a boy or a girl?"

"Is it asleep?"

"He's not going to poop?" asks someone at the table, "is he?"

"I think Luca has better table manners than that," I reply to Zoe's horrified question.

"Oi!" Luca exchanges.

"Whose kid is it?"

That was the one question I've been dreading. And my girl Zoe was the one asking it.

"Is he a relative?" asks Zoe.

"Er she's a relative yeah, well kind of a relative and yeah I was supposed to be babysitting but I didn't want to miss out. I'll get together so here we are." I am aware that I'm babbling.

"How old is she?"

"Oh she's cute."

"Why do you have to do the babysitting?" That one is asked by Max.

"Why on earth did you bring her?" asks Zoe.

"Her name is Rosie." I pick the easiest question to answer first.

"Hi, Joey," Eamon's voice rings out from behind me.

My heart sank. "Oh sweet Jesus! You brought Rosie?"

"Yeah so?" I turn in my seat, challenging him to make a thing of it.

"How come Joey got stuck with looking after his relative's baby and you didn't?" asks Zoe.

I'm glaring at him, narrowing my eyes so he would know I was threatening him.

Somehow the message must've got across because even though he looked distinctly unimpressed, he didn't say anything. It's not that I am trying to hide the truth exactly, I just want to tell my friends about Rosie in my own time, in my own way. Well that's what I am telling myself.

"What brings you over here?" I ask my brother. Not that I particularly care about his answer, I just didn't want him to give the game away.

"Meeting mates for a bite to eat but they haven't arrived yet," Eamon replies, stroking Rosie's cheek with one finger. "Okay if I hang with you guys until they get here?"

"Hell no!" Max snaps, "this is a private party, you aren't invited."

Well, I don't want my brother to hang around with us either but there is too much venom in Max's voice.

"Joey, tell your brother to get lost," Max orders. "He can fuck off."

My frown deepens.

"You heard him," Rory joins in, "get lost."

"Hang on—" I begin.

"Hang on for what?" challenged.

I open my mouth to argue, only my brother got in first. "Joey, don't worry, it doesn't matter," Eamon put a hand on my shoulder, "I'll see you later."

I look at my brother but he isn't looking at me, instead he and Max are regarding each other, the same disdained look on both their faces. Eamon turns sharply and walks away. I turn to my mates. "Max, don't speak to my brother like that all right?"

"What?"

"I said don't speak to my brother like that, okay, if anyone is going to tell him to get lost it will be me, that goes for you too, Rory," I say.

"Sorry Joey but your brother gives me the creeps," says Max.

"What the fuck are you on about, you weasel, why would Eamon creep you out?" I ask slowly.

Uncomfortable silence ricocheted around our group, I could feel Rosie stirring against my chest.

"WELL?" I persist.

"He just does," Max tries to shrug away his comment.

"The way he's hanging around after you and he stares at everyone."

"Staring? What a load of crap, Max."

"Besides Joey, we don't want some little kid hanging around with us and now you bring a second child into our group," laughs Rory with Max joining in.

I look from Max to Rory, "oh yeah very funny, glad I can keep you both amused but I'm telling you now. Lay off my brother."

Luca, Max, Rory and I have been friends a while. Luca and me met in primary school, then we went to the same grammar school and met Rory then Max came to our school at 14 and latched on to our group, don't know why. And surprisingly Luca let him in and he has been a permanent fixture ever since.

But tonight there is something a bit off, how Luca and Rory wouldn't meet my gaze, unlike Max who is staring at me and he accused Eamon of staring.

"Okay Luca, what's going on?" I ask.

"Nothing is going on Joey, come on, you don't want your little brother hanging round us any more than I do."

"You guys need to chill out, you'll wake the baby," says Zoe.

Too late. By the way Rosie is wiggling against my chest, it is already too late.

Then Rosie opens her eyes, takes a second to check out her surroundings, looks up at me and wails the place down. Dammit! I unstrap the carrier and try rocking Rosie in my arms but the music is suddenly too loud and the laughing too loud and the lights too bright and the smell of lager is nauseating.

I look down at Rosie, feeling really bad as I understand how she is feeling, everything far too extreme for her and with that she wails even louder. And I forgot to bring out her baby bag so I had no food, no nappies, no book nothing.

Realisation of how unprepared I am really scares me, I haven't thought about Rosie, I have been only thinking of myself.

"It's okay Rosie, I'm taking you home," I whisper to her as she clings to my shirt, she looks so scared. I should never have brought her in the first place, what a stupid idea.

"God, she's so ugly, isn't she?" Max laughs as he watches her cry.

I look down at Rosie's face all scrunched up, tears running down her face as she sobbed. I feel like my heart has stopped beating, my lungs stopped working for a second and I could feel my rage bubbling up.

"Firstly no one looks their best when they're crying, secondly and more importantly, if you ever call my daughter ugly again, I will hammer you."

I look up at Max, I don't need to stare or glare or raise my voice for him to know I meant every syllable. He has a face like a weasel and he has the nerve to call Rosie ugly. I've glanced around the room and all eyes are on me and Rosie.

Well now I have told him and everyone else about Rosie. I knew I would have to tell them but I thought I would tell them in my own way and this wasn't quite what I had in mind.

"Your daughter?" Zoe is the first to speak.

"That's right," I answer.

"Your daughter?" Luca repeats.

My friends are looking at me like I've just emerged from a spaceship.

Then Luca starts to laugh. "Ha-ha! Good one Joe. You had me going there."

Some of the others also start to laugh, most don't. They are watching me for their queue. One gotcha from me and I'd have them rolling around laughing. One word and I'll be off the hook.

Rosie would be my secret, a family secret. A secret. I look down at Rosie, she is looking straight up at me, still crying. I kiss her forehead before turning to look directly at Zoe. So many things I want to say to her, so many things I want to explain to her in private, not the way I just announced it.

Just for once I'd like my life to run according to my schedule.

"Rosie is my daughter and I'm taking her home. Have a great night everyone."

"Hang on Joey." Zoe is at my side before I have a chance to move, she looks at me then looks at Rosie and looks back at me again. "You weren't joking?"

I say nothing. If this is a joke, then it is on me, not by me.

"Who is its mother?" Zoe enquires.

"Zoe, I really wanted to have this conversation in private with you not in front of all our friends."

"Who is its mother?" Zoe asks more angrily.

I pause for a few seconds. "Amy Hunter."

"Amy?" Zoe's eyes are full of anger. "All this time you were carrying on with her behind my back."

"Zoe, you should know me better than that, Amy and I split up after Luca's Christmas party. That was almost 2 years ago, like the rest of you I haven't seen her since."

"How old is that thing?" Zoe points at Rosie.

I raise an eyebrow, "Rosie is 11 months, she is a year old next month and she's not 'that thing'."

"Okay, I'm sorry but I don't understand. How come you didn't tell me you had a daughter?"

"Only just found out yesterday myself. Amy came round and brought Rosie with her."

"Are you two back together again?"

"No."

Who am I now? I should be at the bar knocking back bottles of lager. My head should be buzzing with plans and schemes and dreams of university and beyond. Now my entire life is filled with Rosie and nothing else.

I could hear the laughter behind me. I just want to get far away from it. And away from all these questions.

"Didn't you know Amy was pregnant?"

"No, I didn't."

"Is that why she left school so abruptly?"

"I guess so."

I really am not in the mood for 20 questions. And the laughter inside the bar is beginning to get to me.

"Where is Amy, why don't you bring her along tonight?"

"She's gone."

"Gone?" Zoe frowns.

"Yes, gone. She went to live with friends and dumped Rosie on me. Amy didn't want Rosie and neither do I but I'm stuck with her," I say. The moment the rotten words are out of my mouth, I want to call them back. I glance down at Rosie and we leave.

As I walk through the bar, I hear, "hey Brophy, I hear you got a sprog now." Out of the mouth of Vincent O'Brien. I turn round to face Vinny (as he is known as).

"Bloody hell, he's only bought the sprog with him." Vinny is killing himself laughing and his mates now joining the laughing too. "You're well and truly fucked now Mr Brophy, how clever are you now?"

"Shut the fuck up O'Brien, at least I'm able to procreate, oh sorry, you probably don't know what that word means, look it up on your phone if you can spell it."

"Brophy, you've got some mouth on you, you better give your head a wobble before I take major offence."

Major offence to Vinny meant smashing the fuck out of you. It's funny how it goes, he's from an Irish family like us and lives down the road. But Vincent always seems to hate me and Eamon, his siblings are always okay with us and his parents are always lovely to us, especially since Mum died.

Vincent O'Brien is 22 and works in the building trade with his Dad. He was never the brightest spoon in the drawer but he always seems to get work and have money in his pocket.

But he has a real nasty streak in him and has always been a bully as long as I can remember. I turn and start to walk away, looking down at Rosie who is still sobbing quietly. I kiss her head and smile at her.

O'Brien shouts, "that's it Brophy, home to bed for you and your wee sprog."

I carry on walking, I can still hear the laughter out here on the pavement.

I have to get Rosie home.

I have to get my daughter home.

20

Joey

My bedroom door opens and Dad puts his head round, he whispers, "I see my little angel is asleep, how was it on your own with her? Obviously it went good seeing your results here," he walks into my room and is staring down at Rosie in her cot.

He leans over the cot and kisses the top of Rosie's head, "night my little angel, night Joey," and he's gone. Phew that was a bit close, only just got in and got Rosie settled and she's only just stopped making little sobs in her sleep.

How could I have been so stupid to take a baby to a restaurant? I just hope that Eamon keeps his mouth shut, when he gets in. Then I hear his key in the door and Dad greeting him, I jump out of bed and run down the stairs in case he tells Dad about me in the restaurant with Rosie.

I could hear them chatting, I walk into the living room, "hey Joe, how was your night?" Eamon asks.

Before I can answer, Dad answers for me, "he's had a great night, Rosie is in bed asleep so he's getting the hang of it, no problem, was it Joey?"

"It was okay," I reply.

"Did you take her out for a walk?" smirks Eamon.

"Don't be mad Eamon, you don't walk that wee buck at night, you're something you are; so how was your night Eamon, did you meet your friends?" asks Dad.

"Yup the four of us had some burgers and milkshakes, mind you they were a bit late so I talked to Joey's mates for a while, they were asking after you Joey, they couldn't believe you missed the night." Eamon is such a wind up merchant and a prolific liar.

I change the subject to stop him going on. "How about you Dad, did you have a good evening? Was Maggie hitting on you again?"

"Jesus, stop Joey! I told you now she's a woman on a mission but I think she wants any of the lads."

"Poor Dad, so you're not the chosen one, you're just one of many."

"You could be her toy boy, I reckon she's about 60 at least," laughs Eamon.

Which makes us all laugh. "Well on that note, I'm off to bed lads, don't be much longer you two, remember our little buck will be up early, nite lads."

I waited till I heard Dad's footsteps going up the stairs. "Were you okay Eamon after I left or did Max start again?"

"No, he was too busy slagging you off but why the fuck did you bring Rosie? What were you thinking?" asks Eamon.

"That's the thing Eamon, I wasn't thinking, well I wasn't thinking of Rosie, she woke up and screamed the place down, so I left."

"Sorry I never saw you leave, just looked round and you were gone."

"Did you see Vinny and his mates not in the restaurant in the bar?" I asked Eamon.

"Yeah seen them when I walked through but thankfully none of them seen me, why?" asks Eamon.

"Ah, he just started trying to wind me up about Rosie."

"He's a right maggot, what did you say?" asks Eamon.

"Just kind told him about himself, which didn't go down too well," I reply.

"Be careful Joey, you know what he's like, he always holds a grudge."

"Don't worry bro I can handle him, I can talk him round." With that we both realise we better head to bed.

I'm only asleep a couple of hours when I'm woken by Rosie screaming and I mean screaming, I try everything to pacify her, I check her nappy which is dry, warm some milk but she doesn't want it, I check her cot in case something was making her uncomfortable but it's fine. So why is she still crying?

My bedroom door opens and Dad asks wearily. "What's going on?"

"I was just coming to get you, Dad," I admit. My words come out slurred, I am so tired. "I need your help Dad, she won't stop crying and it's doing my head in."

"Is she hungry?"

"No, I warmed some milk but she didn't want it and her nappy is dry, what's wrong with her Dad, why is she constantly crying?"

"Joey, your daughter can't talk yet, so how else is she supposed to let you know that something is wrong?"

"Dad, you're missing the point, how on earth am I supposed to know what's wrong with her? I'm not telepathic."

"No, you're missing the point, Joe, you don't need to be telepathic, you just have to listen to her and respond, your mum used to say that you and your brother had different cries when you wanted different things.

"Annie said both of you had a higher pitched wail when you were hungry and more whiny low pitched cry when your nappy needed changing, maybe it's a woman's thing or a mum thing because I could never hear the difference."

Dammit. The last thing I needed at three in the morning is a stroll down memory lane. "How does that help? I still don't know what's wrong with her," I snap.

"What I did Joey instead, as I didn't have your mum's expert ears, was check everything, check your nappy, I'd make sure you weren't too hot or too cold or too thirsty; the point is Joey it's a process of elimination."

"That will take forever," I protest.

"And you're in a rush to do what?" asks Dad, eyebrows raised.

"Sleep," I say, at the moment I would pay hard cash just to sleep.

"Well, unless we find out what's wrong with her then neither of us will be getting back to sleep, so pass her here."

I was glad to hand Rosie over to him, my tired arms flop to my sides. I watch Dad put his hand on her forehead and then onto her cheeks.

"Hmmm."

"What's wrong, Dad? Does she need a doctor? Should I call out the doctor?" I feel myself panicking.

"No need, panic over. She's teething," says Dad as he hands Rosie back to me.

"Wait here, I'll be right back," he comes back grinning and waving a tube of teething gel. "Bet you're glad now I did the shopping," he says winking at me.

Glad? Glad? Right now I could kiss him.

"Sit her on your lap then put a little of the gel on your finger and rub it on her gums but make sure your hands are clean."

Dad squeezed some gel onto my index finger and watched as I applied it as gently as possible to Rosie's gum where I could feel her bottom two teeth are starting to show.

Rosie chomped on my finger as I applied it but it didn't hurt. I guess she wants the pain to stop as much as I did. She is still grizzling a bit and on Dad's instructions, I stand up, hold her close to me and start to sing quietly and dance in the darkness of my room with the glow of the hall light.

Dad waits for me for another five minutes, until Rosie settles down and finally falls asleep. Moving like a zombie, I place Rosie in the cot covering her up to her waist with her baby blanket. Then I sink onto my bed, too tired to do anything else.

"Night son." I am only vaguely aware of Dad pulling my duvet up around my body.

"Night, Dad," I mutter. And I am out for the count.

21

Joey

"Come on Rosie, just a few more mouthfuls," I plead, each of my eyelids feel like they needed matchsticks as I struggle to keep them open.

"Here comes the aeroplane Rosie, open your mouth." But she isn't having any of it and I couldn't say I blame her; she is just as tired as I am but if she didn't eat now, the whole day's schedule would be history.

I know I am supposed to be flexible about these things with a young kid but flexibility and tiredness don't really go together. And it felt like I only just closed my eyes to sleep before it was morning and time to open them again.

"Come on Rosie, please eat some more of this yummy banana porridge." I lean forward and open my mouth to show her how it should be done.

Rosie reaches out and her tiny fingers touch my cheek, I freeze, we watch each other intently. Rosie strokes my cheek and smiles. That's all it is, a smile. Slowly I draw away, feeling strange I'm not sure why.

I finally finish feeding Rosie her breakfast and she is now drinking juice out of her nonslip cup. Next thing Eamon appears at the kitchen door and spins round to leave the moment he got sight of me. But too late. I am on my feet in a second.

"Eamon, what happened to your mouth?"

"Nothing," Eamon pauses before heading back into the kitchen, "morning Rosie," he smiles at her only to wince, his hand flying up to his mouth.

His top lip is swollen and his bottom lip is the red and angry looking. I also notice a bruise on the side of his face.

"Nothing doesn't cut your lips," I frown, "what the hell happened to you? You didn't have that when you came in last night."

"I fell out of bed."

"And what, landed on your face?"

"Just leave it alone Joey, it doesn't matter, I'm alive, aren't I?"

"What huh? What's that supposed to mean?"

"Just tell me what happened, ahh hang on, you went out again, that's why you never got up when Rosie was crying."

"Okay yes, I went out again, I was invited to a party, they wanted me to sing and play guitar for them which I did and then your mate Luca, Zoe and the rest of the crew arrived.

"Which was fine until Max started shouting and heckling me and kept shouting out songs he wanted, basically anything that had the word baby in it you know like BABY BABY, BABY LOVE, I GOT YOU BABE, BABY ONE MORE TIME.

"So I asked him to stop ruining the night for everyone, so then he got up on a chair and started telling the whole room about you and Rosie, saying how the mighty have fallen, so I pushed him off the chair and said look who's fallen now!

"The whole room went mad laughing then he got up and punched me in the mouth and I fell to the floor and hit my head, hence why I look like this, he would've carried on punching me but guess who stepped in?"

"I'm guessing Luca or Zoe."

"No, unbelievably it was the one and only Vincent O'Brien."

"What Vinnie? Are you certain you didn't have too much to drink and got knocked out by the punch and your imagination took over, ha ha ha."

"I'm as surprised as you, Joey and at first I thought I must've taken a blow to my head but Vinny jumped in and took him down with one punch and when he eventually came round for being stunned, Vinnie told him if he laid another hand on me, he'd knock him into next week."

"I don't understand, Eamon."

"I tell you Joey, I was flummoxed, I mean Vinnie but we chatted for ages after and he's really nice when you get to know him."

"He must be up to something Eamon, just be careful."

"I don't know Joey, he seems pretty genuine that's what confused me."

"Listen to me now, I'm telling you again, be CAREFUL."

"Message received loud and clear," says Eamon.

"I really don't know Joey, why are you hanging around with that lot and funnily enough, that's what Vinny said."

"What do you mean by that? They are my mates."

"You let them say and do whatever they want, Joe."

"Like what?" What was Eamon driving at? And what the hell has it to do with Vincent O'Brien.

"Never mind," Eamon sighs.

But I did mind.

"Okay, sometimes they come out with things that make me cringe but they don't mean them, not really, it's just their sense of humour."

"Joey, you only see what you want to see," sighs Eamon, "That's always been your trouble."

"Oh yeah? So tell me what it is you think I'm missing."

Eamon looks at me, shakes his head but doesn't reply.

I change the subject, as this conversation isn't going anywhere.

"So whose party was it last night then?"

"It was my mate Roxanne and I went with Lizzie and Ruby."

Why are most of Eamon's closest friends girls?

"Don't you have any close male friends?"

"I've got male friends, there is Dylan, Zach but my closest friends are the girls."

"Have you decided what you're going to do about your place at university?" Eamon asks before tucking into his yoghurt mix with oatmeal and grapes. {Very good for the skin apparently.}

"No," I admit, "not yet."

"What are you waiting for, divine intervention?"

"No just the postman," I reply.

"What?"

"Never mind." I am not about to tell Eamon I have sent off for a DNA testing kit and was waiting for it to arrive. Dad rolls into the kitchen, yawning, his boxers slung low on his hips. I look at Dad and give him a signal with my eyes to look at Eamon.

He turns around and takes in Eamon's face, "what the hell happened to you?"

"I tripped and fell," says Eamon.

Dad frowns, "don't your bloody eyes work?"

"DAD! D'you mind not swearing in front of Rosie please?" I say. "I don't want her to inherit your swearing."

"Cheeky bugger."

"Dad!"

"OK, OK. Sorry, Rosie, I'll be more careful."

Eamon and I exchange a smile and Rosie starts to giggle.

Dad sits down with his toast, "hello my little angel, you are such a good baby, Grandad loves you so much."

"Good baby? You do remember I was up most of the night with her, don't you?" I say grumpily.

Dad turns to me, "listen to me, Bucko. Count yourself lucky that she's not a new-born, they wake up about every two hours throughout the night, wanting to be fed. Well at least you two guys did. You see these wrinkles round my eyes? Thanks to you two."

"You've got those because you don't moisturise," says Eamon.

"I'd rather me wrinkles thanks," says Dad, "so how are Rosie's teeth this morning?"

"Well, she's not crying anymore but she's still drooling all over me," I say, remembering how soggy my T-shirt was at the time I carried her downstairs for her breakfast.

"Well, she is the only female that would ever drool over you," says Eamon.

He thinks he's so funny.

I hear the click of the letterbox and I head for the door before anyone else can move.

It has arrived. My DNA kit has arrived.

22

Joey

Dumping the other two letters on the hall table, I call out, "I'll be right back," before racing upstairs. I need to be alone once I figure out what I needed to do. Opening the package, I carefully place its contents on my bed.

There are three different coloured collection envelopes, yellow, pink and blue; blue for the Dad, pink for the Mum and a yellow for the baby. How very stereotypical. Luckily for me, this test doesn't require a swab from Amy to establish paternity.

Each collection envelope has details on it that need to be completed before the swab is put into it. As well as the collection envelopes, there are two pages of instructions, 1 reply envelope and three plastic packets each containing two cotton swabs.

According to the instructions, I am not allowed to drink coffee or tea for at least four hours before taking my cheek swab and I have to wait at least two hours after Rosie has eaten before I can swab her cheek.

I could still taste the cup of coffee I've just finished so now I have to wait. Dammit. I read all the instructions and I can choose either receiving results in the post or emailed back to me.

Email is faster but we all share the one computer and I couldn't take a chance of Dad or Eamon getting the results, as they would go ape shit! I just don't want them to know anything about this yet, so snail mail it is.

Now that the test is here, I just want to get on with it. But I would have to wait till just before lunch. Then I have to wait between 4 to 7 days for the results. I think back to the early hours of the morning, it's up and down, up and down, to get Rosie to sleep.

Not even my nights are my own anymore. The funny thing is I find myself watching her, always looking at her. I can't stop.

My daughter, Rosie.

My daughter, Rosie?

"I just need to know the truth," I whisper into the silence of my room.

That's all I want; the truth.

So why do I feel so guilty about doubting that Rosie is mine?

After tidying up the stuff on my bed and hiding it away in my bottom drawer, I look at my mobile which I've left off and recharging all night. It is just a reflex to switch it on. I stuff it into my pocket but the moment I put in my passcode, it starts beeping.

Seven missed calls from a number of my friends and twice the number of text messages. The word has really got round. I push the phone into my trouser pocket before heading back downstairs.

I just reach the bottom of the stairs when the doorbell rings. I open the door, it's Zoe. Well, she hasn't wasted much time.

"Can I come in?"

I stand back to let her pass and shut the front door. We stand looking at each other awkwardly. She leans forward and gives me a brief kiss. I think more to get it out of the way than anything else.

"Joey, are you okay?" asks Zoe.

"Fine." I shrug and think what a stupid question, she knows damn well I'm not.

"How's er—?"

"Rosie? She's fine. She's in the kitchen."

I lead her into the kitchen feeling really uncomfortable. I feel so embarrassed. Zoe is my girlfriend, we've exchanged loads of kisses and the odd grope or two or 20, nothing more and here I am with a kid.

"Hi, Eamon. Hello, Mr Brophy," says Zoe as we walk into the kitchen.

Dad nearly collapses as he is in his boxer shorts. "Hi Zoe, excuse my attire," says Dad,

Looking daggers at me and not knowing whether he should get up or stay sitting, he chose to stay sitting, thank God. And Eamon just nods at her and continues eating his breakfast.

Zoe is looking at Rosie and Dad uses this opportunity to dash out of the kitchen, saying, "I'm just going for a shower, be back soon," glaring at me as he goes.

"Aren't you going to say hello to Rosie then?" asks Eamon.

Funnily enough, I am thinking the same. Zoe looks totally shocked but says, "oh yes, of course, hi Rosie," as she pats her awkwardly on her head. Rosie isn't impressed and I can see she is getting ready to start crying, as she looks up at Zoe. So I grab her out of her highchair and hold her close to me.

I can see Zoe is struggling to say something appropriate. "So this is your daughter."

"No flies on you, Zoe," says Eamon.

The way Zoe—well, let's just say if looks could kill, Eamon would be dead. Rosie wraps an arm around my neck and looks Zoe up and down like she isn't terribly impressed. I have to bite my lip but not Eamon.

"Joey, I think your daughter is pretty smart," he says as he stands up to put his bowl in the dishwasher. "She must get her brains from her mother." At that moment, Rosie begins to giggle and gurgle.

Zoe frowns, "you're not funny, Eamon."

"Rosie thinks I am," replies Eamon.

I have to bite my lip harder as there is something about Rosie's laugh that is infectious. But judging by Zoe's expression, she is immune.

"Joey she looks just like you, I can see that now," says Zoe.

"Oh God, I hope she's not that unlucky," Eamon quips.

"Joey, can we go for a walk or something?" says Zoe. "I'd like to talk in private."

"Eamon, I don't suppose you could—?"

"No, I couldn't babysit," interrupts Eamon.

"Why don't we take Rosie for a walk, maybe to the park," suggests Zoe.

Take Rosie out? In daylight?

"We could take her out in her buggy," says Zoe.

Oh God. Pushing a buggy. I take a deep breath. I mean it wasn't that I was ashamed of Rosie. I wasn't, it was just people are bound to look at me. I look out of the kitchen window. It is a beautiful day with not a cloud in sight, so I couldn't even use the weather as an excuse to stay put.

"Would you like to go for a walk?" I ask Rosie, she smiles at me. I take that as a yes. "I'll be right back," I tell Zoe, "help yourself to a drink from the fridge if you want one."

I go upstairs with Rosie and change her out of her baby grow and into one of her new dresses Dad has bought her. Her legs kick out constantly like she is riding a bike. It is only my super-fast reflexes that stop her kicking seven bells out of my arms. I've put some little socks on her feet and we are ready to go, I hit the landing just as Dad comes out of the bathroom.

"You might have told me that Zoe was coming round this early," says Dad.

"I didn't know she was," I reply.

"Hmmm," Dad is only slightly placated, "are you off out then?"

"Yeah, we are taking Rosie to the park."

"Not without a hat on her head or her sunshade umbrella," frowns Dad. "It's baking out there today, you don't want that wee one to get heat stroke. Where's the pink hat I bought her?"

"In my drawers," I reply.

"Well, I think it would do more good on her head," says Dad.

Rosie has one of the three drawers in my chest of drawers. All my stuff that used to be in there, I've been chucked into the bottom of my wardrobe. I put Rosie in her cot, I went round into the drawer until I found her hat. The moment I put it on her head, she raises a hand to try and pull it off.

"I don't blame you," I tell her, "but we're going out now and it will protect you from the sun."

"Nnuuh, nnuuhg," Rosie tells me.

We head downstairs and Zoe follows me into the sitting room and watches as I put Rosie in her buggy. I check Rosie's baby bag to make sure I have spare nappies and we are ready to go.

"See you later, Dad," I call out.

He appears at the top of the stairs, fully dressed in jeans and a blue T-shirt, thank goodness. "Enjoy your walk."

Zoe opens the front door and we walk out into the sunshine.

I've never pushed the buggy before and it felt, to be honest, a bit strange. We walk in silence for a while. I honestly couldn't think of anything to say—something that has never happened between me and Zoe before.

"I'm sorry," says Zoe finally.

"For what?"

"That you've got stuck with a kid that you don't want."

Zoe was only repeating what I said the night before so why did it jar with me?

"I was stupid, that's all."

"Did Amy say when she's coming back?"

"No, it could be next week or next year or never."

"What are you going to do?"

"I'm not sure, I'm thinking about my options," I say.

"What about university?"

"I'm still hoping to go, but," I shrug. I don't need to say anything else. Silence.

"What would you do if Amy doesn't come back before you're due to start uni?"

I shrug again. "I'm trying to sort it out so that I can still go to uni but it will take a week or two before I know one way or the other what my options are."

"What are you planning?"

"I don't want to say yet," I force a smile, "I don't want to jinx it."

Pinning all my hopes on the DNA test was clutching at straws but it was all I had, if Rosie, if she isn't my daughter, then I could hand her over to Social Services with a clear conscience. But if it turned out that she was my daughter.

"Nnuuu wwunn," says Rosie.

I lean over the buggy, "what's the matter?"

Rosie is kicking out and waving her hands and doesn't look at all happy.

"What's wrong?" asks Zoe.

"I think she's thirsty," I reply.

Well, it was a hot one. The sun is beating down crazily. Rosie is grizzling and quite frankly I can't blame her. It hadn't been my idea to come out in the first place. And we are only halfway to the park and I am already feeling like a wilted lettuce leaf myself, so I can only imagine what Rosie is feeling.

"We could all do with something to drink." I decide.

A few shops further on the High Street is a newspaper shop that sells groceries as well. I swing the buggy round and we all head inside straight for the fridge. I grab a carton of orange juice for Rosie, a can of ice cold ginger beer for me and a Diet Coke for Zoe.

Then we go over to join the queue of people who have had exactly the same idea. A blonde middle-aged woman in the queue directly ahead of us turns round to check who is behind her, I guess.

She looks fed up and bored but the moment she catches sight of Rosie, she is all smiles. "Hello sweetheart," says the woman bending down and leaning in far too close to Rosie's face. I pull Rosie's buggy back slightly. "She's gorgeous," the woman smiles at me, "and doesn't she look like you."

How I wish people would stop saying that.

"Hmm," I reply.

"How old is your sister?" asks the woman.

"Er?"

"It's not his sister, it's his daughter," Zoe provides. Why on earth did Zoe volunteer information the woman hadn't even asked for?

The expression on the woman's face changes dramatically. Her eyes are wide, her mouth open with shock. "She is your daughter?" she asks scandalised. She doesn't say it quietly either. More people in the queue turn round. My face begins to burn.

"She is your daughter?" The woman repeats, even louder than before just in case there is someone in the country who hasn't heard her the first time. "How old are you?" she continues, her eyes narrowing.

None of your business, that's how old I am, I thought to myself. I glance at Zoe. She is looking down embarrassed. "Well?" The woman persists.

"Seventeen," I say reluctantly.

Instant facelift. Her eyebrows almost hit her dyed blonde hairline. "Seventeen!"

Oh my God, everyone in the shop is truly shocked; they seem to be all looking at us.

The woman looks Zoe up and down like Zoe isn't much.

"Don't look at me like that, it's not my baby," Zoe proclaims. "I'm just a friend, he has nothing to do with me."

I look at Zoe, taking in the indignation in her face, her lips are downturned and she looks angry. One glance reveals only too clearly that the blonde doesn't believe her.

"Unbelievable, kids having kids," the woman sniffs, "and no doubt you're not working and you're living off benefits."

"It's none of your business what I'm living off." That last comment makes me snap.

"It is my business when it's my tax money that's providing your child benefit and jobseekers allowance and whatever else it is that wasters like you get from the state."

"Excuse me? How dare you!" She isn't really saying what I think she is saying, is she?

"Seventeen with a kid," she says shaking her head.

"For your information, I don't get a damn penny off the state," I say furiously.

"Joey, just leave it," Zoe says as she places a hand on my arm but I am so bloody angry I just shrug her off.

"You don't know a bloody thing about me, so where do you get off talking to me like that?"

"Look, I don't want any trouble in my shop," the shopkeeper comes out from behind his counter.

"Leave him alone," pipes up a woman behind me. I spin round to see who is speaking. It is a brunette lady with a tired face and she is holding the hand of a small boy about six or seven years old. "At least he's in his child's life, at least he hasn't done a runner like a lot of men do." The brunette puts an arm around her boy to pull him closer as she speaks.

The words should've made me feel better but they don't.

The blonde lady who is giving me a hard time purses her lips and favours me with one of her last filthy looks before she turns away. People in the queue ahead of her regard me with varying degrees of disapproval.

"What? Anybody else like to say something? Anyone else like to comment on my life," I ask, spitting out words of intense resentment. I just wish Dad was with us, he'd eat them alive.

They all make a great show of turning to face the front. And all I want to do is punch the living daylights out of something. Or someone. And all I want to do is hop on the first train, destination anywhere, with just the clothes on my back and nothing else.

And all I want to do is drop into a supermassive black hole and disappear. It hits me like a ton of bricks. I am in a lose-lose situation.

Ironic that when I saved up and bought my phone, it came with all kinds of information. When Dad bought a family computer, it had been packaged up with all kinds of instructions.

When Amy dumped Rosie on me, there was nothing. No menu, no briefing, no crash course, nothing. I am doing my best but if Rosie stays with me, every person I meet would feel they can comment or condemn or criticise.

And if Rosie goes away, it would be the same people saying how terrible I am for giving her up. No matter what I do, no matter how hard I try, it will never be enough.

23

Eamon

Some days, memories wrap round me and keep me warm and safe. And some days, memories wrap around me and are as sharp as rusty barbed wire. How come the same memories bring two such completely different feelings? Today, I'm thinking of my mum and it hurts.

24
Joey

In spite of every instinct telling me to go back home, I don't. Am I really going to let some idiotic old biddy ruin my day? The verdict is already in on that one. Three streets and not much chat later, we reach the park, which makes pushing the buggy a lot easier.

On the way there, I have to walk out into the road at least three or four times because of inconsiderate gits that have parked their cars on the pavement, making it impossible to pass with a buggy. Before Rosie, I would never even have noticed this. Now I want to key each car barring my way.

When we reach the children's playground, I put Rosie in a baby swing after checking it carefully to make sure there is no way she can slip out. Then I push her gently back and forth. She loves it, laughing with pure abandonment.

I smile as I listen to her pure joy over a little thing like a baby swing. As Rosie's laughter washes over me, the storm that is still raging inside begins to fade and die. I look around the playground, noticing all the other kids having fun.

It has been quite some time since I've been here. Listening to the laughter and the shouting brings back memories of how much I used to love this place when mum used to bring us, strange that I should've forgotten that.

It wasn't that I haven't considered having a wife and children of my own someday, it is just one of those things I considered inevitable like having a mortgage and paying your taxes.

But I always thought this would be 10 or 15 years in the future, then I'll have no trouble doing it. No trouble at all. It isn't Rosie who is wrong. It is just the timing.

My lousy timing.

"This feels strange," says Zoe.

"Yeah, I know," I agree.

We stand together yet apart.

I carry on pushing Rosie. I look at Zoe and ask her, "are you gonna tell me what happened last night?"

Zoe asks, "What do you mean?"

"You know exactly what I mean, when Max smacked Eamon in the mouth."

"Max was only joking and Eamon took offence and pushed him and he fell on the floor, not much more to say," smiles Zoe. "OK. You were mentioned," laughs Zoe.

"I bet and I'm glad you find it so amusing, so what was said about me?"

"Oh, not much really," Zoe answers, "just surprised about you having a kid and reckoned you were a bit of a dark horse and some people thought it was just a wind up."

"And that was it?" I can tell by the way Zoe shifts from foot to foot and is unwilling to meet my gaze that there is more to this. "Zoe, there's something you're not saying, just tell me," I demand.

"Look Joey, it was no big deal. Rory made a comment about your brother and your kid."

"What kind of comment?" This was turning to hard work, trying to get the information out of Zoe.

"He said that living with Rosie was probably the closest Eamon would ever get to the opposite sex but don't worry, Eamon told him where to go."

"Rory said that to Eamon?"

"Eamon was walking past our group and Rory started up, you know what he's like when Max is around but Eamon gave as good as he got."

Dammit, that's what I am afraid of.

"Stop worrying, Joey. Eamon is more than capable of taking care of himself."

"You reckon, have you seen the state of his face?"

I know Eamon has a tongue like a razor and is as clever as a fox and my money is on him to win any arguments. But not all arguments we're fought with sentences. I needed to have a word with my brother.

And I really don't understand the animosity towards my brother from Rory and Max and what was Luca doing when all this was going on, having a sleep?

"Joey, what happens if," Zoe's voice snaps me back out of my thoughts.

"Yes?"

"If Amy doesn't come back at all?"

"I really don't know," I reply.

Silence.

"Joe, what's wrong with me?" Zoe asks quietly.

"Huh? What do you mean?"

Zoe takes a deep breath, "how come you had a kid with Amy but you never wanted more than a kiss and a cuddle from me?"

What is she serious? Where Zoe had trouble meeting my eyes before, she is looking straight at me now.

"You never said you wanted to take things further."

"You never ask, Joey."

"Would you?" I glance down at Rosie.

"Would you have wanted to, if I had asked?"

"I also don't know Joey, I mean I wasn't given the chance, was I? So again, I ask what's wrong with me, Joey."

"I swear Zoe, there is nothing wrong with you."

"Then how come you slept with Amy but not me?"

"Zoe," I sigh, "it's not that simple."

"Explain it to me then."

God, this is so uncomfortable.

I am silent for a few moments, as I try to form an explanation in my mind. To find the right words. "Zoe, do you remember Luca's party after Christmas a couple of years ago?"

Zoe nods.

"Well, that's when it happened between Amy and me. We were both drunk and it was kind of over before it started." I can feel my face heating up with embarrassment, I really don't want to say any more than that.

Zoe nods again to show she understands. "That was the one and only time," I say, "and it was nothing to write home about but you and me; well, I wanted it to be special and I thought when we were at uni together with our own rooms, we could take our time to get to know each other intimately."

114

"I see," says Zoe, "but what about her?" As she points at Rosie, "what are your plans now?" asks Zoe.

"My plans haven't changed, I still want to get my degree and make something of my life."

"And if I can't join you?" It is really unfair of me to ask but I need to know.

"Joey, I like you. I really do but I'm going to university, I'm going to have a career. I've got plans, I want to have a life. All this," Zoe points again at Rosie. "All this is a bit overwhelming."

For me too, doesn't anyone recognise that? But I get the message, this is not what Zoe had signed up for.

"I understand," I say and I do, my lousy timing has struck again.

"It's not fair that you should have to give up all your dreams for something that wasn't planned or wanted," says Zoe, anger lending an edge to her voice.

It wasn't that simple, the something she is first referring to is a someone. That I am currently pushing in the swing, as someone who has kept me up most of the night but as someone who only has to laugh to make me smile. A real living breathing person and that has made all the difference.

Zoe said, "There must be something you can do."

I shake my head. "I don't see what," I reply. "Rosie doesn't come with an on off switch that I can use for the next three years to get my degree."

We spend another half hour at the playground, I hold Rosie upright all the way down the baby slide and we do that a few times.

I place her on the baby seesaw holding her hand, Zoe pushes the other end up and down and the whole time Zoe and

I discuss uni, schools, friends, politics, even the weather—but not Rosie. And there is no more talk about the two of us. We head home after that. I invite Zoe inside but she declines.

"I have a lot of stuff to sort out before I leave for university," she says.

I say nothing.

"I'll phone you soon, okay?" says Zoe.

"Okay," I kiss Zoe goodbye, feeling this will be the last time ever; she and I would occupy different worlds from now on.

I go indoors, the cool quiet of the house is more than welcome. I unfasten Rosie from her buggy and I take her straight upstairs, closing my bedroom door firmly behind me. I swab her cheek, I swab my own.

I leave the swabs balanced 2/3 on one third of my desk so they can air dry. Rosie sits on the carpet exploring rather than reading one of her picture books. I sit on the bed and watch her as I wait for my old life to return.

Rosie looks up at me and smiles, before returning to her book, I look down and try to figure out exactly what I am feeling but I have to give up. When the swabs are dry, I place them in the collection envelopes and seal them before placing them in the reply envelope.

Time to head out again. I will just wash my hands, then we're off to get this done. In the bathroom, I stare at myself in the mirror above the sink, is it my imagination or is my face thinner? I wasn't eating regularly.

I just snack here and there when Rosie is taking a nap. And by the time she is in bed, I am too knackered to bother eating. Looking after a kid is a 24/7 deal. There isn't a hell of a lot of room for anything else.

116

I am just drying my hands when a strange sensation comes over me. My bedroom door. How—did I shut my bedroom door? I step out onto the landing to see Rosie crawling towards the top of the stairs and she is crawling fast!

"ROSIE!"

Rosie turns towards me but her hands are past the top so now she was going to pitch herself forward.

"ROSIE!" I've never yelled so hard or moved so fast.

Rosie cries out but her body tilts forward, I snatch her up and it is only sheer luck that I don't trip over and fall down the stairs with her in my arms. Rosie is wailing now and God knows I know how she feels.

"ROSIE, DONT EVER DO THAT AGAIN!"

She bawls even louder at that. I am not helping matters but I have to shout over the sound of my own heart thumping. I feel sick. I am so lucky to get to her in time but now I am actually feeling physically sick.

My head is filled with images of what might have happened, all because I've left my bedroom door open. I half collapsed, half sat down on the landing, Rosie still in my arms. I rocked back and forth slowly while dragging air back into my lungs.

"I'm sorry Rosie, I'm sorry." The words are softly spoken and heartfelt. It isn't her fault. I am the one who left my bedroom door open. I hug her even more tightly. "I am so sorry."

Dad appears at the bottom of the stairs. "What's all the shouting about?"

I now know what Dad means when he says every time Eamon and me got in serious trouble, it took five years off his life, that is after he has finished shouting at us of course.

"Nothing Dad," I answer as I stand up, my legs wobbling.

Dad frowns at me, "are you sure you're alright, son?"

"Yeah, I'm fine." Still clutching Rosie to me, I head back to my room. I need to buy a gate for the top of the stairs as soon as possible. The cost will put a dent in what is left of my money but no way am I going to go through that again.

The envelope containing the swabs lies on the bed. I sit down next to it, rocking Rosie in my arms until she quietens down. Snatching up the envelope, I make tracks while holding Rosie firmly.

There will be no more accidents or incidents.

Less than a minute later, Rosie is back in her buggy and I am pushing her towards the nearest post-box. But for some reason, I hesitate. I look down at Rosie who is trying to eat her own toes, I look at the brown A5 stamped envelope in my hand and still I hesitate. What the hell is wrong with me?

This isn't about her or me, I tell myself, this is about the truth and of course, I've already paid a whole heap of money and I can't afford to bottle it now. I force myself not to think of anything except pushing the envelope in the post-box. And it goes.

I am doing the right thing.

Aren't I?

25

Joey

It's around seven and it looks like it's gonna be another hard night with Rosie, I think her teeth are playing up again. I rub some baby ointment on her gums and the hard shell of her emerging two bottom teeth but it doesn't seem to make much difference; they seem to be really giving her grief and if she's having grief, then we're all having grief.

I've paced up and down, I have lifted her high. I sing to her, I dance around the room with her but nothing seems to work and it doesn't help that my phone would not stop ringing.

I haven't replied to any of the messages or texts on my mobile so my friends have resorted to using the landline. By the time Dad has taken the fifth message, he is getting pretty pissed off.

"Joey, I'm not your PA," he tells me, "next time, you answer it."

To top it all, the doorbell rings. As I'm already on my feet, I head for the door.

It is Auntie Mary.

Dammit! The family grapevine is working overtime. Rosie takes one look at my aunt and cries louder. Clever child, she always makes me feel kind of sad too.

Mum and Auntie Mary had been twins, they are not identical but close enough for me to see Mum every time I looked at Aunt Mary but their looks have been the start and end of the similarities. Mum had been honey whereas my aunt is vinegar.

And by the look on my Aunt Mary's face, I am about to get both barrels. Auntie Mary looks Rosie up and down. "I see the news is correct, you've been a busy boy." She is going straight in with the verbal uppercut to my chin.

Rosie is squirming in my arms. I am terrified I am going to drop her, I try putting her down on the ground but she isn't having any of it and she cries hard and grabs round my neck and hangs on. I place her back against my shoulder. Auntie Mary gives Rosie a long hard look before turning her attention back to me again.

Here it comes, I thought, bracing myself.

"Can you say the word 'contraception' or is that too many syllables for you to handle?"

Right hook to the temple.

"Hello Aunt Mary," I say faintly. I doubt she even heard me over the sound of Rosie crying, which is probably just as well. The tone of my voice would've given far too much away.

"I seriously thought you had more about you Joey, I thought you were the sensible one," says my auntie.

Left jab to the stomach.

"But like 99% of men, you don't have enough blood in your body for your brain and your willy to function simultaneously."

I think my blood has turned to lava, I could feel my face and my whole body burning up with embarrassment.

That was a knockout blow, I'm down for the count.

"Right, give me that wee Bucko (Irish for little one)," Auntie Mary holds out her hands.

I am not keen on handing Rosie over to Auntie Mary but my aunt was not a woman who took no for an answer. Auntie Mary gently touches Rosie's hair and strokes her cheek, before resting my daughter against her shoulder and gently jiggling her but Rosie is still crying.

"What's wrong with her?" asks my auntie.

"She's teething."

"Ah! It's yer old toothy pegs, honey?" she says to Rosie. "Well I'm over twenty and my teeth still give me Jip, I'd happily pull them all out if I don't need them. Joey, you look tired."

"I am, I'm totally cream crackered," I admit.

"Get used to it."

Stupid me, for a brief moment I'd actually thought she was starting to feel sorry for me.

Then Aunt Mary places a free hand under my chin and gives it a squeeze.

"Sure, listen now honey, don't beat yourself up. Yes, you were careless but you were also damned unlucky."

I wait for the trip wire. None appears, so I try to smile but it doesn't quite reach my face.

"Just you hang in there, okay?" says my aunt. "All of this must be totally mind blowing for you, just take one day at a time darling."

"I'm trying, Aunt Mary but it's hard." I couldn't speak above a whisper any louder and I think I would burst into tears. I could feel myself getting choked up.

"And Rosie has everyone's attention?" asks Auntie Mary with a smile.

Her words surprise me. "Something like that," I admit.

"Listen here now Joey, from what I can see you're doing a grand job, just hang in there."

"But Auntie Mary what happens if I muck up?"

"Don't you think every parent worries about exactly the same thing?"

"Do they? Even when they're old and in their 30s?"

Auntie Mary smiles. "Oh yes, even when they are that old. Listen Joe, d'you want a bit of advice?"

I nod warily.

"You just do your best, love. That's all any of us can do. If you can look at yourself in the mirror and know you did your best, then you're ahead of the game."

"Auntie Mary, how come you never had kids?" I ask.

"Oh Joey, I was desperate to be a mum. I got pregnant four times but each time I had a miscarriage."

"Oh, I didn't know. I'm sorry," I reply, "did you decide to stop trying after that?"

"After my fourth miscarriage, I was told I'd never be able to have children, that's when my ex walked."

"That's why you and Uncle Paddy got divorced?" I say shocked.

Auntie Mary nods.

"What a bastard."

"No Joey," Auntie Mary smiles sadly, shaking her head, "no, he wasn't, he was just as desperate to be a dad as I was to be a mum but he could walk away from the situation and I couldn't. That's just the way it is Joey, some get to walk away some don't."

Auntie Mary and I look at each other, in that one moment, we understand each other perfectly.

"Mary? You should've told me that you were coming round," Dad emerges from the sitting room.

"I need to give you a warning now, do I?"

"I didn't mean that the way it came out," sighs Dad.

"Why are you still out here in the hall?" asks Dad.

"I'm talking to my nephew."

"Mary, the lad doesn't need one of your lectures," says Dad.

"No but maybe the truth would help him instead?"

"What do you mean?" I ask.

"Yes Mary," says Dad, drawing himself up to his full height and muscle pulsing in his jaw.

"Why don't you tell us what you mean?"

"Auntie Mary, what's going on?"

"Jack, don't be so sensitive," Auntie Mary tells Dad, "all I meant was that you can help Joey, if he gives you a chance because you had to bring up him and his brother alone for the last few years, so he can learn from you."

It takes a couple of seconds but Dad relaxes slightly and Auntie Mary does the same, taking her cue from him.

"Oh, I see."

He might, I don't. There is definitely something not quite right going on.

"Look, you two, we do have chairs. Why don't you chat sitting down?" says Dad.

"Mary, will you take a cup of tea?"

"I'd love one," says my aunt.

Dad heads off towards the kitchen.

"Have you and your Dad had a heart-to-heart about all this?" Aunt Mary lowers her voice to ask.

"About all what?"

"About how you're feeling, how are you're coping."

"Come on, of course not, girls do that not guys."

Auntie Mary shakes her head, "Joey, you are so like your father."

"No, I am not," I deny. Eamon had said the same thing and I didn't appreciate it then either.

Auntie Mary gives me a knowing smile, "here, I think your daughter would rather be held by you."

She hands Rosie back to me, to my surprise Rosie settles against my shoulder and does indeed quieten down. Making sure she is secure in my arms, I lean my head against hers briefly. Mary gives me a significant look. I straighten up, moving my head away from Rosie's.

"What?" I ask.

"Joey don't underestimate yourself," my aunt tells me.

"What do you mean?"

Auntie Mary sighs, "I remember how withdrawn you became when your mum died, I think Annie's death made you wary of change."

"I'm still not with you," I frown.

"All I'm saying is, don't let the past make you afraid of getting to know your daughter."

Is that what she thinks is going on? If so, then she has it all wrong. I am not about to argue with her. We head into the sitting room.

"Hi Auntie Mary," Eamon springs up and gives our aunt a hug. Eamon does that kind of stuff so much easier than I do.

"Hey Eamon, how's life treating you?" asks Auntie Mary, her eyes narrowing as she notices his cut lip and face.

"Fine, Auntie Mary."

"Well now, Eamon are you going to explain your face? A terrible split lip and a bad bruising on the side of your face."

I hadn't noticed the bruising down the whole side of his face had got worse, it must've come out overnight.

"I'm waiting, either you or Joey need to tell me what's going on."

"It's nothing to do with me," I reply.

"OK OK. Don't stress Joey, I just fell over, Auntie Mary."

Auntie Mary frowns, "so you fell forward and split your lip then rolled over and bruised the side of your face? Come on Eamon, surely you've got a better story than that, come on what's the craic?"

Both I and Eamon laugh, we look at Auntie Mary whose face is very straight, next thing she bursts out laughing as well, "okay Eamon, let's park it there. I can leave it to my imagination."

And we are laughing again and now Rosie has joined in giggling away which makes us all laugh more.

I got to say it feels good to laugh.

"What's the craic in here, I could hear you laughing from the kitchen?" Dad says as he appears with a tray with mugs of tea and cake and biscuits.

"Hey Dad! Did you nip out and buy a tray? Can't remember seeing it before," says Eamon teasing Dad.

"Cheeky bugger, if you ever cleaned the kitchen, you might come across it," Dad snipes back.

"Now now, lads," Aunt Mary says smiling.

I put Rosie down on the floor and she is off like lightning; crawling, exploring, finding her favourite rabbit, who she put straight into her mouth. Then she crawls over to the sofa and pulls herself up next to Auntie Mary.

She looks at Mary and smiles. Auntie Mary has received Rosie's seal of approval. Next thing before any of us know it, Rosie has let go of the sofa and was standing on her own.

"This wee lassie is going to walk, call over to you Joey, coax her."

I am scared she might fall and hesitate.

"Come on Joey quick," says Auntie Mary urgently.

"Rosie, Rosie, come to dada, come on Rosie, look what I have?" And I hold out her favourite book.

Next thing before any of us could say anything, she is off coming towards me, those few steps seem like a mile to me and the next thing she is standing between my legs, smiling and giggling.

"Isn't that wonderful? She walked to daddy." Auntie Mary claps and seems as pleased as me.

It suddenly hits me. "MY DAUGHTER."

Now I wish I hadn't sent off the DNA swabs, this is my daughter!

Dad and Eamon are praising Rosie and she seems to know she has done good and is smiling at everyone, then she takes off again towards Auntie Mary, as Mary is holding her rabbit, "come on Rosie," she encourages.

I am walking behind her now just in case. But she doesn't need my help, she holds the sofa, turns and smiles at us all, then she starts clapping with Aunt Mary, which makes Mary crease up with laughter.

Once again, Rosie has brought everyone closer. Rosie is making me confused about my feelings. I need to be alone, so I grab a mug of tea and head upstairs, I can feel them all looking at me but I need space.

26
Eamon

I roll over, I put the pillow over my head, then the duvet but nothing is stopping Rosie's wailing penetrating my ears! At this rate, I'll have bags, no suitcases under my eyes by morning.

I have a constant headache since my run in with Max, I didn't tell Joey but I was actually knocked out when I fell, I didn't want Joey jumping off the deep end, he has enough on his plate.

That's it. I can't stand anymore, I jump out of bed and head for Joey's room, why has he just left her crying like that?

I mean, what is he doing? Is he even in there? Poor Rosie alone in her cot, I push open the door not bothering to knock and there is Joey, gently swaying and singing to Rosie and Rosie is having none of it, she is struggling to get free and still roaring the place down.

"How much longer is this going to go on for?" I demand.

Joey's stunned stare rapidly changes into a blood-freezing glare. "Are you fucking kidding me?" he asks, his voice rising with anger.

I pull a face, I am beginning to think I might have been a bit hasty, "well, I'm sorry Joey but how am I supposed to get to sleep with this racket going on?"

"And how are you going to sit down ever again, once I've finished kicking your fucking arse?" Joe asks. And his expression told me he was mere seconds away from carrying out his threat.

"Do you want some help?" I offer.

"If you can stop her crying, I'll give you anything you want," says Joey.

"You look half dead on your feet," I tell him.

"You try walking up and down and dancing in the dark with a crying baby for two hours, see how you would look," Joey snaps.

"Maybe you're holding her wrong?" I suggest but I truly didn't have a clue.

"Why don't you get over here and show me how it should be done?" snaps Joey.

"Because Jack Brophy only raised one stupid son, not two," I tell him.

I only just made it out of his room before one of his pillows just missed me.

Joey has the last laugh though, as Rosie's crying keeps me awake for another hour.

I am exhausted, half asleep, I promise next time I pass a pharmacy, I would pop in and get Joey some condoms.

27

Joey

Over the next few days, I tripped and fell into a kind of routine. My days and nights and even my thoughts all now belong to Rosie. The daily routine Dad had written out for me turns out to be a lifesaver.

And I kind of tell myself I know what I am doing, well sort of. To be fair to Rosie, she's not bad compared to stories I've been told about other babies. Maybe this is because she isn't a new-born.

I'm not saying Rosie isn't hard work because she sure to hell is, I have to be on the ball 24/7 as she demands constant attention. Amy hadn't just dumped a baby on me, she also dumped a straitjacket of anxiety on me, which couldn't be removed.

I am constantly questioning every decision I make. Is she too hot? Is she too cold, am I over feeding her or under feeding her, is she getting enough exercise?

The list just goes on and on. Was anything enough?

Every day I think I am messing things up but in spite of everything, Rosie continues to keep smiling and laughing and when I pick her up, she clings to my neck like I matter to her.

And when I blow raspberries on her tummy, she laughs like it is the funniest thing ever. Now she has found her feet, she toddles everywhere and is into everything.

It is a constant battle to keep up with her and to make sure she doesn't hurt herself or break anything. Just now I found her trying to force her rabbit into the DVD player, how she managed to get it to pop open is a mystery.

"No Rosie, naughty, you mustn't put poor bunny in there," I tell her, snatching the bunny from her and the DVD player.

With a look of surprise, then she scrunches up her eyes and opens her mouth and wails.

I say, "Look Rosie, daddy is using bunny as a football," and I head it. "Or Rosie, you can you wear it on your head," and I walk up and down like a model on the catwalk. That seems to do the trick, she is now giggling, thank God. Major incident avoided.

"Something you want to tell me?" Eamon quips from the door.

I turn round, the rabbit flies off my head. Eamon gives me a round of applause. Giggling, Rosie joins in clapping her little chubby hands. I bow to my fans.

Not a day passes without me having to fix something that Rosie has 'redesigned'.

Rosie also seems to have a fixation with Dad's slippers, she always seems to be carrying one. I caught her dipping one of Dad's slippers in the downstairs loo. I rinsed off the slipper and put it back in the hall, hoping that by the time Dad got home, it would have dried out and he wouldn't notice.

One time, I was watching her bashing two of her farm animals against each other, all the time chatting away in her baby talk to them. Every now and then, she would look round and smile at me. And as I watch, I realise that Rosie and her antics are getting to me.

I have to stop myself from laughing too hard with her infectious giggle or smiling at her too long. I know I'm letting her inside my head too much. I don't want her inside my head.

My life is already spinning round so fast that I have no idea which way is up anymore. My thoughts and feelings are all over the place and with each passing day, it grows worse, not better.

And on top of all that, Eamon was up to something.

Most nights, he leaves the house around 7:30 to 7:45.

If it was once or twice, I wouldn't have noticed but this was every night. And he doesn't get home till 10 or 10:30. It was rare for Eamon to be out every night. Dad has to work late to try and pull in a little bit more money to help with Rosie, so he isn't around to question my brother the way I would've liked.

So it is down to me.

"Where are you off to? Again?"

"Out," Eamon replies.

"I gathered that, out where?"

"Out, out."

He is starting to really annoy me, more than usual.

"Eamon, where are you going?"

"How is it any of your business?" Eamon frowns.

"In case anything happens to you," I argue.

"And how will knowing where I'm going stop anything happening to me?" asks Eamon.

"So that's it is it, you're not going to tell me?"

"Joey, Rosie is your child, not me," says Eamon, "I'll see you later."

And that's it, he is gone out the door.

Why is he being so secretive? I shake my head, Eamon is right. Rosie is the one who needs looking after, not my brother and if he wants to play the man of mystery that is his business.

The days when I am home alone with Rosie are the most nerve racking, even though Dad phones on the hour every hour to make sure everything is okay. I don't know whether I should resent his regular check-ups or be grateful for them.

But this constant not knowing what to do next is doing my head in. I have to make some hard decisions. I can't afford to waste any more time dithering. It isn't fair on Rosie for a start. And even though I now have a kid, that doesn't stop me from trying to hold onto some of my old life but it doesn't seem to be working.

I have phoned Zoe numerous times but all I got was her voicemail. I tried phoning Luca but he has plans every night of the week so he couldn't come round. A few of my other mates like Ricky and James did drop by to see me but Rosie demanded and got most of my attention so they didn't stay long.

My so-called close friends are busy during the day and I couldn't go out at night, not without being able to guarantee Dad would be home in time to babysit and it wouldn't really be fair on him as he is working so hard.

Saturday morning again, waiting for the postman; this time for the DNA results.

It's here! One look at the white envelope, I instantly know what it is, I take deep breaths one after another as I try to steady my galloping heart. Why is it affecting me like this, I mean this is what I want—proof positive that Rosie is my daughter or not. And it has arrived at last. I stand looking at it.

"Joey, open the bloody envelope," I tell myself. And yet it remains unopened in my hands.

"An gg goo aags," Rosie is calling me from her high chair in the kitchen.

I've got the envelope and three more that came with it and head back to the kitchen, I dump them on the work surface as I go to see what is wrong with Rosie.

She has dropped her spoon on the floor. She doesn't actually use the spoon; only to hit her bowl, her chair, her head and anyone that would pass by.

But Dad has said it didn't hurt to start early so she got used to the feel of it.

Talk of the devil and Dad walks in, "morning Angel, morning Joe," yawns Dad as he comes in the kitchen.

"Hi Dad," I reply.

"An nnuyaang," says Rosie.

Dad walks over to the baby and kisses the top of her head. He dotes on her already. I take Rosie's spoon over to the sink to give it a quick wash before handing it back to her. It is another warm sunny day outside.

Maybe a bit later, myself and Rosie will go to the park. Rosie really enjoys it there. And recently, it seems girls like a man with a baby even in most cases they thought she was my little sister.

The girls strike up conversations with me and it is nice to talk to people my own age. So having a baby has some perks. And Rosie loves the swings. So it is a win-win for both of us.

"Joey, what is this?"

Dad has a white sheet of paper in his hand, one glance at the other unopened letters on the work surface tells the whole story.

"You opened my letter?" I accuse.

"It said Mr Brophy on the envelope," says Dad.

"It said Mr Joseph Brophy."

"Sure, you know yourself I was opening them on autopilot," says Dad.

"What is this anyway?"

"Why are you asking me a question that you know the answer to?" I reply sharply.

I close my eyes briefly. So much for not getting the results by email in case it got intercepted. And I can't see myself bluffing my way out of this one. It's great, isn't it? Dad gets to know the results before me, ironic huh?

"Joey?"

"Stop that, you know what it is, you've read it," I say.

"Not all of it," Dad denies. "I read enough to know it's not mine but not the whole thing." He'd obviously read enough to get the gist of it though.

I straighten up and look directly at Dad, "I sent off for a DNA test, those are the results."

"YOU DID WHAT?" Dad asks me, astounded.

"I needed to know for sure."

Dad just stares at me. "Sure, look Joey, anyone with half an eye could see Rosie is yours."

"I needed to know for sure," I repeat.

"Still trying to wiggle out of your responsibilities? Is that what this is all about?" Dad's tone is scanting. "And if this test tells you Rosie is your daughter, are you going to be pleased or disappointed?"

"Honestly Dad? I'm not sure what I will feel." And I wasn't lying, I really didn't know how I would feel but I'm going to know very soon.

I don't think Dad heard a word I said, I've seen Dad angry but nothing like this. His whole body is held rigid and his lips are clamped so tight they have practically disappeared.

"I'm not trying to get out of anything," I say quietly. "I just wanted to know the truth."

"The truth? Here's a news flash, the truth isn't going to bend itself to suit you."

"I know that."

"Do you, are you sure about that, are you? Because from where I'm standing, it looks like you'd do anything to get rid of Rosie, for starters what are you doing about your university place or have you already accepted because you reckon Rosie is not my granddaughter and will no longer be a problem before term starts."

We regard each other with varying degrees of dislike.

"Dad, it's obvious you really don't think much of me, do you?" I say.

"I'm not the one trying to find an excuse to get rid of my own child."

"Neither am I," I tell him.

"What's this then?" Dad waves the DNA results under my nose.

"I haven't even read that yet," I remind him. "You opened it not me."

Dad's eyes narrows but I continue on, "and for your information, I've already withdrawn my university place two days ago. And I cancelled my student loan."

That surprises him, "you did?" Dad stands there staring, regarding me. At last he has stopped waving the sheet of paper around. "Why?" he asks.

"Because I realised I couldn't go to uni and look after my daughter." I shrug. "I had looked into crèches and nursery places for Rosie while I attended uni but I soon realised I don't have that kind of money.

"If I've got a job in the evenings and at weekends to pay for nursery place, who would look after Rosie while I worked? I think she had more than enough of being moved around in her life already."

"You really gave up your university place?"

"Yes, I did."

"You knew didn't you, what the DNA results was going to be?" asks Dad.

"I'm not psychic, Dad." I smile faintly, "but everyone says she looks like me and she laughs like Eamon and she's stubborn like you, so she's definitely a Brophy. I don't need a piece of paper to tell me that."

Dad looks down at the DNA results in his hand. "Maybe you should read this?" He holds out the sheet of paper.

I take Rosie out of the highchair and cradle her and kiss her on the forehead, "you tell me what it says," I say holding Rosie actually tighter.

A silence descends over the kitchen, the only sound is my heart beating.

Rosie is a Brophy, I am 99.9% sure of that but the remainder 1% of doubt gnaws away at me. And now as I sit in the kitchen, my heart pounding, sweat beads on my forehead, I realise I am afraid.

But which result am I more afraid of? Rosie is my daughter or that she isn't? Dad is reading the sheet of paper, his lips are moving, why can't I hear what he's saying?

"Pardon?" I say.

"Rosie is your daughter," grins Grandad. "It's confirmed. I could've told you that, in fact I believe I did!"

"Nnnggghh," says Rosie.

I relax my grip around her, I don't need to hold her quite so tightly. I smile at her, kissing her cheek, Dad is still blabbering on about how I wasted my money and how I should've just listened to him. Rosie.

My daughter.

My daughter, Rosie.

"Rosie," I say softly. "I'm your daddy, say 'Daddy'."

28

Luca

Max really hates Eamon, I know he has strong opinions about black people, about foreigners but regarding homosexuals, he is off the Richter scale.

Joey and I have been friends for a long time but he's changed, not just to do with him having a daughter; actually that's quite funny. But like Max says, he really thinks he's something; it's always been, I'm going to be a journalist, I'm going to pass my exams, he's never had any doubts and as Max says, what are the Brophy's doing here, why don't they fuck off back to paddy land?

And Joey always knew I fancied Zoe but that didn't stop him going after her, even though it seems he had Amy in the back pocket as well. I'm in love with Zoe and I think Joey having a baby has split them up. Which I'm really pleased about, now maybe I can make a move on her.

Eamon is a real gay prick. He's a mouthy little fucker who hangs around with girls, going shopping with them. And he lets them paint his nails, you would think he would try to keep a low profile about his sexuality but oh no, not Eamon; it's like he loves shoving it in our faces. Max reckons he's going to give him a slap if he doesn't stop acting the big I am.

29

Eamon

So Joe thinks that I'm up to something.

In fact, I'm not really up to anything.

But I have met someone, how is it possible be so happy and so miserable at the same time? When we are alone, he is great, he's thoughtful, generous and smarter than I thought and he makes me laugh so much.

But that's when we are alone. Then he is wonderful.

He is teaching me to box so I can learn to defend myself and I'm teaching him guitar.

I wish he wasn't ashamed of me and if he could stop being so ashamed of himself, then maybe we might stand a chance.

I don't understand as he hasn't told his family that his sexual preference is guys.

But then I haven't told my dad, Joey knows but he thinks I will grow out of it.

What a Muppet!

30
Dad

Being a Grandad is a strange affair, I love Rosie and I haven't said it to Joey but I see his mum in Rosie. And finally he stopped messing about and he's really doing well with her.

Sure look, I know I don't tell him he's doing well but it's the Irish way I think, I can never remember being praised but I suppose that doesn't make it right. I must try harder and try telling him how great he's doing.

Gotta be careful though, he might collapse in shock.

Eamon is being a bit evasive, I must find out what's going on with him.

I've been so focused on Joey and Rosie, I kind of dropped the ball with Eamon. He's a good lad but his wit and his tongue are so sharp I'm surprised he hasn't cut himself but he's also very witty and I reckon the split lip and the bruising down the side of the face was no fucking fall unless he fell off a horse.

I'm not blind to the fact that he's also, I think, struggling with his sexuality, so I hope this beating wasn't anything to do with that because people can be cruel and unaccepting.

If I'm right about him, then he has a hard road ahead of him.

31

Joey

Dad has left long ago for work and Eamon is off to school saying he'd be a bit late back as he was going to check out a college or something, so it is just me and Rosie. The autumn morning is overcast but still warm.

"Do you wanna go to the park, Rosie?" I ask. Rosie waddles over to her buggy. I have my answer!

I carry Rosie upstairs and she doesn't seem that heavy and I smile at her as I open the stair gate thinking since the DNA results, I now could wear the truth like a bespoke suit and make proper decisions.

And why I gave up my university place before I knew the DNA results is a mystery to some people but not to me, Rosie needs looking after no matter what. That's all there is to it. Giving up my place at university didn't mean I couldn't go next year or the year after that or sometime in the future.

There was just one problem. Money!

I couldn't keep expecting Dad to pay for everything. I had to step up somehow financially but let's think about that another day, it's now time for Rosie to have fun at the park.

Sitting Rosie on my lap, I gently put on her soft furry boots, they remind me of UGG boots that every girl seems to be wearing and some boys these days. They have a strong sole so I figured we would walk to the park and have a run round once we get there.

That way she'd be good and tired after lunch and have a proper nap.

It isn't quite so nerve wracking looking after her anymore, at least not in the same way as before. I mean, when she starts crying for something and I can't figure out what it is, it does require lots and lots of patience which I didn't know I possessed.

The one thing I didn't expect was the loneliness. Some of my friends came round to see me but once the novelty wore off and the curiosity had been satisfied, they stopped calling. Most days, it is me and Rosie until Dad and Eamon come home.

We walked around the shops and to the park just to get us out of the house, otherwise I would've gone crazy. It seems life is going on around me but my life is on hold.

But I have Rosie.

Buggy in one hand and Rosie's hand held firmly in the other, we head out of the house.

"The park, here we come," I tell Rosie.

She looks up at me and smiles. But we are less than halfway there when the sky turns very dark and the rain starts chucking down. We are both drenched in less than a few minutes.

In my head I am cursing, I mean even my underwear is getting soggy! Rosie, however, loves it. She walks through puddle after puddle and laughs like a drain. It obviously feels so good, she pulls her hand free from mine and splashes through it again and again and again, laughing her head off. Who would've thought a puddle could be so entertaining?

The rain is getting heavier and I am worried that maybe there would be thunder and lightning, so I grab Rosie and strap her back into her buggy. And I take off running with her and we head for home.

When we are at last indoors, I dry Rosie off and change her clothes. I don't want either of us catching a chill. I change my T-shirt and pull off my damp socks, then we head upstairs. After a kiss on the top of her head and making sure that she is safe in the sitting room, I head into the kitchen to start the laundry.

I am just putting some of those wet clothes into the washing machine when the doorbell rings. Straightening up, I found I wasn't expecting anyone but it would be great to talk to anyone.

I open the door.

"Hello, you must be Joey."

I look at the woman on my doorstep. She is a few centimetres shorter than me, black hair tied in a ponytail and she is wearing a green skirt suit with a white blouse. She is carrying an outsized bag over her shoulder. I haven't a clue who she is.

"My name is Diane and I am a social worker, may I come in?"

What on earth is she doing here? "First door on the left." I indicate, she goes into the sitting room, stops when she sees Rosie playing with her toy animals.

There is a distinctly pongy whiff wafting up from her. Her nappy needs changing. She sits down on the sofa and I sit down on the chair opposite her.

"How is she?" Diane asks. "Rosie, isn't it?"

"Yes, that's right and she is fine," I reply.

I don't know what to do now; should I change Rosie's nappy now or wait until Diana leaves?

I just have to wait until Diane leaves. Rosie plays on the carpet between us and I wait for Diane to get to the point.

"So how are you?" she asks.

"Fine thanks but I'm guessing you didn't come out just to ask how I am?"

"Just so we are clear Joey, as I said my name is Diane and I am a social worker but I am also your girlfriend Zoe's sister and she told me you are struggling with Rosie and that you've given up your place at uni."

I have a bad feeling about this.

Every cell in my body goes on red alert. "Yeah, she told me she had a sister who was a social worker," I reply carefully, "I didn't join the dots when you arrived. I was wondering where all this was leading."

"Sorry, Zoe told me that your ex-girlfriend turned up with a child," she glances at Rosie. "And now you find yourself having to cope with a child alone?"

"I'm not alone, I've got my father and my brother Eamon, who both love Rosie and help with her," I say, "what is this all about? Why are you here?"

"Don't worry, this is an unofficial visit. I've just come to see how you're managing, so Zoe mentioned that you were deeply unhappy."

"I got over it, it was just a shock at the time." I'm getting over it would've been more like it but she didn't need to know that.

"But it can't be easy?" Diane suggests.

I shrug, saying nothing.

"As I said, I'm here in an unofficial capacity but I do have a duty of care to make sure that Rosie is in a stable safe environment."

My blood ran ice cold in my veins. "What are you implying?" I ask. "What did Zoe say to you?"

"Zoe only repeated what you had told her and the baby is a daunting prospect for any new parent even when the child is wanted, you're only seventeen and Rosie wasn't," another swift look at my daughter, "well, she wasn't a life choice you deliberately made, now was she?"

I say nothing. I am only too aware of all the landmines she is throwing around me, just waiting for a word out of place to set them off.

"I understand that you're trying to find a way out of your current situation?" Diane continues.

"I'm afraid you've been misinformed," I reply. "Rosie is my daughter and my responsibility. I'm not trying to find a way out of anything."

"I know you withdrew your place at university, so what do you intend to do now?"

"I'm going to find a job to support Rosie."

"And who will be looking after your daughter when you are working?"

How dare she stick her nose into my business? I bit back what I really wanted to say with great difficulty. I am only too aware that this woman has the power to make it her business but with each passing second, I resent her more and more.

"I'm looking for an evening or night work so Dad can look after Rosie."

"What kind of work?"

"I don't know. I'm still looking?"

"And what if Rosie is sick and your Dad has an appointment and you're at work?"

"I would do what any parent in a similar situation would do," I reply. "I'd come home to look after my daughter."

"Hmm. I am not being funny, Joey but are you even close to coping?"

"What's that supposed to mean?"

"I know that Rosie's nappy needs changing but I don't see you making any moves to do anything about it," says Diane.

"I know Rosie's nappy needs changing but I didn't realise you'll be staying so long, otherwise I would've changed her before now."

"Don't let me stop you," Diane says.

What is this, a test? I tell myself to calm down, don't let her get to you.

I hesitate for a moment then I take Rosie's baby bag off the handles of her buggy and I set about changing Rosie's nappy without saying a word to Diane. The resentment I feel must've somehow got through to her; as I fasten Rosie's nappy, she says, "Joey, I'm on your side."

It doesn't feel like that though.

"So you've decided to keep Rosie with you?"

"She's my daughter," I reply. "I think that says it all."

"Joey, have you really thought this through?"

"Are you serious?" I ask, "I thought of nothing else, I've only had Rosie a few weeks and yes, she's turned my world upside down and I'm still learning and adjusting but I also know I love her and could be a good Dad if given the chance."

"You're seventeen, Joey, you can't be expected to have the patience or attitude for this that an older parent would have."

I am not having that. "There are plenty of older parents who abuse their kids. There are plenty of older parents who don't give a damn about their children and let them fend for themselves, I know I'm only seventeen, I can't help that but I'm eighteen in a few weeks' time and all my family not just me are determined to make this work."

"I'm glad to hear it," says Diane, "because if I feel this is not the best environment for Rosie, there are a number of steps I can take."

I stand up. "Are you talking about taking my daughter into care?"

"That would be a last resort, there are quite a number of steps before we ever get to that point."

But I hardly hear her, I pick up Rosie hugging her to me. She rests her head on my shoulder and starts sucking her thumb.

"Tell me something," I ask bitterly, "would we be having this conversation if I was Rosie's mum instead of her dad?"

Diane frowns, "I don't see how that's relevant."

"Isn't it? You're automatically assuming that because I'm Rosie's dad not her mum, I'm failing. Well, let's talk about her mum. Amy was the one who didn't even tell me she was pregnant.

"Nor did she bother to let me know I had a daughter when Rosie was born. Amy arrived here, told me she didn't trust herself with Rosie and was afraid of what she might do, she gave Rosie to me and did a runner, she's the one who has disappeared somewhere with no forwarding address and yet you're here trying to condemn me?"

I want to shout but I don't. God knows that's all I want to do. How dare she make assumptions about me?

"I can see I'm upsetting you." Diane stands up.

"Of course I'm upset, you stand there threatening to take my daughter away from me for no other reason than my age and my gender. I think if you come here again, you should make an appointment, not just turn up on hearsay and I would like my father and my brother present so you can see us as a family, not just a case number."

Diane scrutinises me, "Joey, believe it or not, I am on your side. This really isn't an official visit and I can see that you're already bonded with your daughter. And I'm here to do whatever I can to help but this requires a commitment from you for at least another eighteen years, think about it."

"You presume I haven't thought of these things, well I have and like I said, I'm already looking for a job."

"It's not just your employment Joey, there are a number of other factors to consider."

"What then?"

"Like where does Rosie sleep?"

"In a cot at the foot of my bed," I inform her.

"And in five years' time, where will she be sleeping?"

"Huh? What a ridiculous question, I don't know where I will be in five years' time, do you know where you will be in five years' time? But I do know if I am still living here with my brother and father, she will have her own room, how many children nowadays are all sleeping in one room sometimes that includes their parents."

"It's not just that," says Diane, "have you taken her to your GP for a check-up? Have you even registered her at the doctor surgery? There are numerous things that need to be sorted out if you're planning on having your daughter stay with you for any length of time."

"I will do whatever is necessary but Rosie is staying with me. I'm not letting you or anyone else take my daughter away from me," I tell her.

"Look, I'm gonna leave my number, if you need advice or help, just call," she digs into her handbag and produces the business card. I watch as she scribbles her mobile number on the back. She holds out the card me and I take it.

"I have another appointment but let me stress, we do everything in our power to keep families together. I really am on your side."

"Yeah, right."

"Your daughter is beautiful," Diane smiles at me, "and doesn't she look like you."

I say nothing.

"Bye Rosie." Diane put out a hand to stroke Rosie's cheek but I move us both away from her and lead the way to the front door. Open it so she would have no trouble leaving, she holds out a hand but I don't take it.

"Take care of yourself and your daughter," says Diane.

"I intend to."

"Myself or one of my colleagues may be back within the next few weeks for a chat with you and your dad, we will make an appointment but just to let you know, we don't have to, we can just come to see how you're all doing."

Thanks for leaving the last comment ringing in my ears.
Is that a threat or a promise?
Either way, I am in trouble.

32

Joey

"Stop panicking."

"That's easy for you to say, Dad!" I am practically shouting down the phone at him, "you weren't here, it was absolutely awful, it was like she was trying to catch me out."

"Joe, she told you it wasn't an official visit, so calm down."

"But this Diane still came, didn't she and she still questioned me; what if she tries to take Rosie away from me?"

"You're getting way ahead of yourself son, the social worker said that would be a last resort, let's face it; the authorities would only take a child if it was in danger and our Rosie is as safe as houses with us and if anyone did try and take our angel, they would have me to deal with and I tell you now, I won't be messing about."

That makes me feel calmer.

"Thanks Dad but I'm still worried."

"I know Joey and I know me telling you not to worry won't make any difference but wait till I get home and we can have a proper talk."

All sorts of thoughts popped into my head, phrases like 'on the at risk register' and 'family court'.

When I think back only a couple of weeks, I was at the computer looking into foster care and adoption. I don't even recognise that person now. What was that saying? 'Be careful what you wish for because you might just get it'. I take a deep breath, trying to follow Dad's advice. Keep calm.

"Joey listen, don't let this woman rattle you, I've got to go but if you want me to come home just say, I'll be there in a heartbeat."

"You would do that for me?"

"Of course Joe, listen if you change your mind just call me, I've gotta go, bye for now, bye-bye bye."

It feels good, to know Dad has my back. For the first time, I thought what this must be like for him. It couldn't have been easy for him bringing up me and Eamon on his own when Mum died, working, paying a mortgage and all the bills, plus keeping us two happy, I know Auntie Mary helped Dad, she used to look after us when Dad worked.

And now instead of two of us, there are three, three that Dad has to provide for and has never moaned about it, he has just taken it in his stride. I have to get work pronto to help out. This has to work for all of us. But first things first, I have a phone call to make.

"Hello?"

"Zoe," I take a deep breath, trying to hold down the anger at the sound of her stupid voice. "I've just had a visit from your sister," I say as quietly as I can muster.

"Joey, how are you? I've been meaning to call but been so busy getting ready for uni."

"I said I just had a visit from your sister Diane," I repeat a little louder this time.

"Oh that's good, she did promise to go and see you."

Another deep breath, this isn't working. I can feel the anger rising, "you told your sister. A social worker about Rosie and me? Why would you do THAT?"

"Oh yes, of course," says Zoe, she seems surprised that I even asked the question.

"I told her how you weren't coping and that you really wanted to go to uni but now because of that baby being forced on you, everything was up in the air for you."

"Why would you do that?" Words are coming out faster and harder. Take a breath Joey, I'm saying to myself, just chill, don't lose it.

"Look Joey, I was trying to help us. This way the baby can be taken care of by a foster parent and you can get your life back," says Zoe.

"I've only seen you three times since she arrived on the scene, she is stopping you from doing all the things we had planned and I miss the way things used to be."

"Zoe, she has a name—Rosie, her name is Rosie and she's my daughter."

"Not from choice Joey, you didn't even know about her till she arrived dumped on your doorstep."

I have to restrain myself from answering for a few seconds to calm myself down.

"What exactly did you tell your sister?" I ask when I could trust myself to speak.

"I only told her what you told me," Zoe replies, "that Rosie has been dumped on you and you didn't want her."

"You have no fucking right!" I shout.

"Excuse me?"

"You heard me Zoe, you had no right to poke your big nose in my business. YOU HAD NO RIGHT TO

INTERFERE and YOU SET YOUR PITBULL OF A SISTER ON ME! JUST BECAUSE YOU WERE FEELING NEGLECTED," I say shouting now.

"Joey that's not why I did it, I was trying to help you—"

"Help! By letting your pit-bull of a sister take Rosie away from me?"

"But you don't want her—"

"Zoe, get this into your thick skull because I'm only going to say this once. Rosie is my daughter and she belongs with me. She is staying with me. If you don't like that, then tough. Tell your bloody sister I'm coping just fine and both of you can keep your bloody noses out of my business, enjoy university."

I hang up. Within seconds, the phone is ringing. I pick it up and put it straight down.

Hopefully now she'll get the message.

"Come with daddy, Rosie." I hold out my hand, "let's get you a drink." Rosie waddles over to me and takes my hand without hesitation. Her hand is so small and tiny and warm in mine. We share a smile as I lead the way to the kitchen.

I pop Rosie in her highchair, I pour out some diluted blackcurrant juice into her beaker. I stay and watch as she drinks it. I feel my eyes starting to well up, I must have grit or dirt in them.

"You're not going anywhere Rosie, you are staying with daddy," I tell Rosie softly. "I promise I will never let anyone or anything change that."

33

Eamon

I can't do this anymore.

What I am isn't wrong.

How I feel is nothing to be ashamed of but that's how he's making me feel.

Why did he even ask me out?

It was his idea for the two of us to get together, not mine but I think he sees me as some kind of spotlight shining down on him mercilessly and drawing too much attention to him.

I want to live my life out loud. But he wants me to whisper through life just like him.

He wants to live his life in the shadows, hoping no one will notice him.

I don't want to live my life like that, I will be seventeen in a few days. I want my life to be fun and open not hiding and lying.

Problem is I really like him but I think it's time to call it a day. I never realised it before but this is my worst case scenario.

This will never work until he learns to be happy with who and what he truly is. One thing I know for sure, it's beyond anything I can say or do to persuade him to accept and love himself and God knows I've tried. I've even suggested counselling.

And I'm starting to get fed up waiting.

I know Dad and Joey aren't sure of my choice. Girl or boy but maybe tonight is the night to put them straight.

34
Dad

Isn't it funny how things turn out? There was Joey not wanting to get involved with his baby daughter and now he's in love with her and wouldn't give her up for the world.

In fact, we're all in love with her and there's no way we will ever lose her. She is our family. I know Joey was very frightened today after the visit from the social worker. And to be honest, it kind of banjaxed mw as well.

We all read horror stories where children are taken off parents and put into care and later on, it turns out to be a wrong decision. But I can tell you now, no granddaughter of mine will ever be taken from us.

35
Joey

Myself and Rosie are up and out early and we are third in the queue at my doctor surgery waiting for it to open. A sign on the door says buggies have to be left in the porch area, so as soon as the doors open, I take Rosie from the buggy, hold her hand while holding the buggy with my other hand.

I must say I'm getting quite good at that manoeuvre. When we get to the reception desk, the lady says, "Can I help you?"

"Hi, yes. I'd like to register Rosie here with a doctor please."

Rosie is looking up at the reception with avid interest. "Are you already registered here?" asks the receptionist.

"Yes, I am." I give her my name and address watching as she stares at the screen.

"And how old is Rosie?"

"She'll be one next Tuesday," I inform her.

The receptionist frowns at the screen before turning to look at me, "do you have her NHS card, her birth certificate and her Redbook on you?"

"Huh? Er. No, what's her Redbook?"

"The book of her medical details to date." I look blankly at the receptionist so she elaborates. "It has information in it like all the vaccination she's had, the birth details, that kind of thing and I'll also need photo ID and proof of address from the person registering her."

"I don't have any of that stuff." I shake my head. "I thought you only needed her name and address and date of birth."

The woman behind the desk gives me a sad smile. "I'm afraid not, maybe you could get your mum to come in and register her once she's got all the appropriate documents together?"

"My mum is dead," I reply.

"Oh." The woman looks suitably embarrassed. "Well, how about your dad? Would he be able to come in or register your little sister?"

Oh God. Here we go again.

"Rosie is my daughter, my Dad is her Grandad," I say trying to keep my tone even.

"Your daughter?"

I sigh inwardly. "Yes my daughter."

"And you," Reception turns back to the screen, "you're seventeen."

"Actually, I'm eighteen in three weeks."

"Right, maybe her mother could come in with the necessary documents, I'm sure she will have them to hand."

"Are dads barred from doing this kind of thing then?" I ask impatiently.

"No. Of course not, I didn't say that, it's just the mother usually has all the documents."

"Rosie's mother isn't around anymore," I explain resenting the fact that I have to explain. "I look after my daughter and all I want to do is register her with a doctor."

"If you could come back with all the things I mentioned then there should be no problem," says the receptionist.

By which time all I want to do is repeatedly bang my head on the reception desk.

I turn and head out. "Well Rosie, this is going to be a right royal pain in the butt," I tell her as I reassemble the buggy and place her back in it.

"Ranngghh baadudf," Rosie agrees smiling up at me.

When I get back home, I go through all the documents Amy has left behind. I should've done it before. Got it! The red book with gold writing on the front, personal child health record.

Inside the numerous pages are various other sheets of folded papers, one of these gives the baby's delivery details. It seems Amy had been in labour for 7 hours and 52 minutes and she just suffered blood loss and a tear.

Bloody hell. It sounded terrible. And who had been with Amy when she gave birth or had she been alone? No one should go through something like that alone. Why didn't she tell me, give me a chance to wrap my head around the idea and step up.

I should've been there not just for Rosie's sake and Amy's but for my own as well. Maybe she thought I would try and persuade her to have an abortion? Or she thought I'd wash my hands of the whole situation.

I look down at Rosie sitting on the carpet playing with a rabbit. I honestly don't know. I carry on looking through the book and there's a whole heap of stuff that I am clueless about.

I promise myself to look up on the Internet all the things I don't understand so that I would know what I'm talking about. Flicking through the book, I saw all the immunisations that Rosie has already had. She is due for her next one between 12 to 14 months old, which I didn't know about till now.

There are development charts, weight and height graphs, pages of help and advice and a couple of pages of comments at the back of the book, which I think were made by a nurse. It isn't much when you get right down to it but at least it filled in some of the gaps.

I made a list of immunisations, work, a place at a nursery, check out local schools and development milestones. I need to get my act together and sort all these things out if I want to keep my baby. And I do. More than anything in this world.

36

Eamon

This is mad! I just wish he'd stop phoning me, texting me and bombarding me with emails and messages. He's driving me nuts, it's getting to the stage where I'm scared to turn on my phone.

It's over.

Why can't he get the message? Does he think this is easy for me?

Does he know this isn't what I wanted?

I was seventeen three days ago and he bought me the most amazing guitar that I have been saving for. I just wish he understands he's allowed fear to take over his life.

So now I'm giving him what he wants, his straight as a ruler, boring as hell life.

Most of me, wants him to leave me alone. But the other part of me wants him to come forward and love me forever.

37

Joey

Eamon is now officially seventeen, so as we were both born in the same month but different years, we were both seventeen for a couple of weeks before I turned eighteen.

But today is about Rosie, it's her first birthday, complete with a cake and one candle. We sing happy birthday to her and help to blow the candle out. She loves it so we have to do it again and again and again.

And she loves the toys and clothes she got as presents from my dad, my aunt and my brother. More farm animals and alphabet blocks from dad, also a pink dress with a matching cardigan from Eamon and money from Auntie Mary.

It's kind of mad though when you think Rosie, myself and Eamon are all born in the same month. Expensive time for Dad.

Eamon takes out his guitar and plays baby songs to Rosie, she claps her hands and giggles and tries to sing along. She particularly loves a song by, I think, Bob Dylan or maybe Tom Paxton called Jennifer's rabbit, which Eamon changes the words to Rosie's rabbit.

"Rosie slept in her little bed

With dreams of a rabbit in her little head
Rosie's rabbit, brown and white
Left the house and run away one night.

Along with a turtle and a kangaroo and seventeen monkeys from the city zoo.

And Rosie too."

I must admit Eamon has an amazing voice and Rosie adores Uncle Eamon.

Dad gets out his camera, knocks off the dust and starts taking photos of us all. It feels like old times and brings back happy memories. And it is good to see Dad laughing with Auntie Mary and smiling; again he takes pictures of us all, Rosie on my shoulders, Rosie with Auntie Mary, Rosie with Eamon and his new guitar (which must have cost him an arm and leg.)

You name it, Dad wanted a photo of it and of course Eamon loves being in the limelight, turn the camera on him and he sparkles like champagne. But even he stepped aside so that Rosie could take centre stage and we are all buzzing around her like bees and she loves it.

Auntie Mary surprises us all when she starts singing. Mind you, it was probably something to do with the Jameson's Dad kept plying her with. Off she goes.

"My young love said to me, 'my mother won't mind and my father won't slight you for your lack of kind and she stepped away from me and this she did say it will not be long. Love to our wedding day.'"

This was one of my favourite songs as my mother used to sing it to myself and Eamon, I wonder if Eamon feels the same about it. Auntie Mary continues on but now Eamon has joined in, which probably says he does feel the same about the song as me.

"As she stepped away from me and she moved through the fair and fondly I watched her move here and move there. And then she turned homeward with one star awake like a swan in the evening moves over the lake.

"The people were saying, no two ever were wed but one had a sorrow that never was said and I smiled as she passed with her goods and her gear and that was the last I saw of my dear."

I look over at Dad and I notice a tear running down his cheek, the song has obviously reminded him of Mum, Eamon and Auntie Mary must've also noticed that because they stop singing the song before the last verse and pretend they can't remember the words.

All along Rosie is doing her own kind of little dance and also singing along in her own little baby talk. I think we have another singer in the making.

It is a great first birthday for Rosie.

Two weeks later, it is my 18th birthday.

I didn't want a cake or any fuss and I said don't get me any presents, just buy something for Rosie if you want to spend money. I have no plans to do anything for my 18th as now it doesn't seem important anymore.

But Dad put his foot down, "Joey, you and your brother go out and enjoy yourself, it's your birthday for God sake. Go and have a meal, see a film, my treat."

"I can't, what about Rosie?"

Dad raises an eyebrow, "I'll babysit."

"I am still worried about Diane the social worker, what about if she hears I've been out."

"Stuff Diane," Dad replies, "it's your birthday Joey, you're only eighteen once and it doesn't make you a bad person to have an evening out with your brother once in a while, go and enjoy yourself. Eamon, take your brother out to remind him what a good time feels like."

He digs into his pocket and pulls out a load of notes, he pulls off a few notes, "go on, you two off and have some fun," he insists.

I am not too sure about this. I pick Rosie up and explain to her, "daddy is going out but only for a little while, I'll be back very soon."

"Jaysus Joey, you think you are leaving the country, you're going out for a couple of hours, Rosie will be perfectly fine with me, go!"

Then the doorbell rings, Dad goes to the door, its Auntie Mary, "happy birthday Joey," she shouts she then hands me a card and a present.

"Thanks Auntie Mary."

"Don't thank me yet Joey, you haven't opened it," she says laughing.

I open the envelope first as Mum had always told us to do so. A cheque flutters out and falls to the floor. I bend to pick it up before Rosie gets hold of it. As I do so, I see the amount on the check. "Jesus Mary and Joseph! I can't accept this Auntie Mary."

"Show me, Joey," says Dad and Eamon in unison. Dad gets hold of it before Eamon. And Eamon perches on the arm of Dad's chair.

"£1800!" They say together.

"Mary, he can't accept such a large amount of money."

"I can," says Eamon laughing.

"Jack, it's not yours to refuse and Joey, shut your mouth. I see you're getting ready to argue about this, sure look I could've bought you something but I figured you could spend this anywhere you want," she says winking at me. "Now open the wee present, Joey."

I unwrap the small box she has given to me, then I open the lid of the box and inside are condoms. I start to laugh and can't stop. I pass the box to Dad and Eamon and they both start laughing along with Auntie Mary.

Next thing, we hear Rosie giggling away, she stops, smiles at me and says, "Dada."

We all stop and look at Rosie and she says again, "dada," and starts laughing again.

I pick her up and throw her in the air, "daddy's girl, did you hear Rosie, she said Dada plain as day."

They are all smiling and telling Rosie how clever she is.

I turn to Auntie Mary. I hug her tightly. "Auntie Mary, thank you so much but it's far too much."

"Sure look Joey, I've got a few bob and you buckos are like my own, so that's that."

"Right, make me a cup of tea, I'll have that and then I'll be off," says Mary.

"The lads are going out for a birthday celebration," Dad states.

"Okay so, just us for tea then," says Mary.

"Listen before you go Joey, I got something I want to give to you," and Dad hands me a box, I open it and it's a gold coloured watch on a black leather strap.

"Dad, this is lovely, it's an Omega sea master, it must've cost a fortune."

"Joey, your mum gave that watch to me on my 18th, I can't wear it, too many memories and I know she'd love you to have it and I don't know how she afforded it."

I could see Dad's eyes welling up, which makes my eyes well up. "I don't know how to thank you Dad, if you're sure you want me to have it, it would be an honour to wear it."

I give him a hug and we both pat each other like men do.

I and Eamon make a break for it to get upstairs to get ready as Auntie Mary could talk the hind legs off a donkey.

To be honest, it feels quite good leaving the house. Rosie walks to the door with Dad and Auntie Mary to see us off. "Say bye to Daddy and Uncle Eamon," he tells Rosie.

"Wave to daddy."

"Dadada," says Rosie waving at me.

"Bye Rosie, see you soon." I wave back. I really wasn't sure about this and I am just about to turn round and go back when Eamon grabs my arm dragging me away.

"OK," I agree reluctantly.

"YES!" Eamon leaps up and punches the air. Turning to me with a huge smile on his face and a glint in his eyes.

"What?" I am instantly on my guard. "What are you up to?"

"Nothing," replies Eamon like butter wouldn't melt.

"Whatever it is, just don't embarrass me, okay?"

"As if," replies my brother but his eyes are saying something different.

"Where are we going to go?"

"I think we should just pop and have a bite to eat at the lemon tree," replies Eamon.

That is okay with me because it wouldn't be too far from home in case Rosie needs me.

169

The lemon tree is insanely busy for a Tuesday evening. We are told there would be a 30 minute wait for a table, I am more than ready and willing to try somewhere else but my brother insists we stay here.

So we park ourselves in the bar and Eamon is trying to get himself an alcoholic cocktail, like that is going to happen! Dad would kill me. I am legally allowed to drink but don't want to, so I order a lemonade.

Eamon sits drinking his virgin cocktail and I try to talk to him about football but Eamon doesn't know a football from a bowling ball, so I soon give up on that. Eamon starts talking about some new singer he has seen on TV who is number 10 in the charts and according to Eamon, he is a useless singer.

And that he is far better than him, so he should make it as well. Then he starts to discuss some designer and my eyes start to glaze over.

Then we go onto the exploits of some Hollywood star. I am struggling to find a subject we can both chat on so I chose music as Eamon could talk non-stop about it.

"Hey, Joey."

I swivel round on my seat, Luca Rory and Max are a bit behind us, waiting in the queue to be seen and seated. I am surprised to see Luca. He has applied to do politics and economics at university and as far as I am aware, has achieved good enough grades to get in, so what was he doing here?

Rory has found a job at electrical company, doing an apprenticeship. I wasn't sure about Max.

"Hey guys," I say.

Eamon speaks to Luca and Rory and then turns and says, "hi Max."

Max doesn't even look at my brother, let alone acknowledge him, instead he says, "Joey, I haven't seen you for a while."

Eamon turns back to his virgin cocktail looking troubled.

"Max, my brother said hello to you," I frown.

"I know I heard him," says Max.

"Then don't bloody ignore him," I say.

"Joey, leave it, it's okay. Really," says Eamon.

But it isn't. "Eamon, I'm sick of Max treating you like dirt," I tell my brother.

"Oh, for God's sake, hello Eamon. How's it going? Happy now, Joey?"

"Ecstatic." Max's attitude towards my brother is really pissing me off. I wouldn't let anyone treat my daughter like that and no way is anyone going to treat my brother like that either.

"What's up with you lot, chill guys," says Luca.

"So Rory, how's electrical business?" I ask. "And what the hell happened to your hair, did you have an electric shock?" Rory's hair is usually brown and long, it is now short spiked up and bright orange.

"I fancied a change," shrugs Rory, running his hand over his head. "What do you think?"

"Do you want me to be honest?"

"No, don't bother," says Rory rolling his eyes.

Of course Eamon has something to say. "I think you look like road kill or a fox that's been electrocuted."

Oh God! When will he learn to keep his gob shut? Rory looks at Eamon like he wants to flatten him.

I quickly try to change the subject to defuse the situation. "So Rory, is there any shift work at your electrical company, as I'm looking for work."

"Are you kidding? You wanna work nights, you must be cracked but no they don't do shift work."

"What about you, Luca?" I ask. "I thought you were off to uni."

"No, my grades were crap, so I'm going to work in my Dad's business," Lucas replies.

"Oh I see."

I turn back to see Max staring a hole through my brother. And Eamon is doing his best ignoring him.

"You okay, Max?" I ask.

Max's attention snaps back to me. "Yeah I'm fine, what have you been up to, Joey?"

"Looking after my daughter Rosie."

"What else apart from that?" says Max.

I think about this question and I realise it isn't worth answering as he wouldn't understand, like I didn't when I asked Amy the same question when she brought Rosie around. Thinking about it now, I'm lucky she didn't head-butt me because you don't know until you walk in their shoes.

"So what brings you guys out here tonight?" asks Luca.

"We're celebrating Joey's birthday," Eamon replies before I can stop him.

"Happy birthday," says Max.

"Yeah, happy birthday," say the others.

"Thanks." I turn back to my lemonade, hopefully they would take the hint and head back to their place in the queue.

"Do you guys want to join us?" Eamon shocks me by asking.

I am glaring at Eamon, waiting to see their response. Luca is grinning like it is the best idea ever. Rory is watching Max, who looks just as uncomfortable as I feel. Max doesn't want to join us, no more than I wanted to join them.

"Yeah, okay," says Luca before Max or I could find a reasonable excuse.

What the hell is Eamon playing at? Why on earth has he invited him to join us? He doesn't even like Max.

We have to wait an extra fifteen minutes because there are five of us instead of two.

They have to push two tables together. Max is seated opposite Eamon, I sit with him on one side of me and Luca on the other. Rory sits next to Max. After a while, the conversation starts to improve and before long, we are laughing and joking just like old times.

At first it isn't too bad but of course they are knocking back lager like it is water. By the time our starters come, they are well on the way to being drunk.

Lager before starters, lager after starters; by the time the mains arrived, chips have been thrown round the table like insults. I feel so embarrassed. I look around, we are the focus of a lot of attention and if looks could kill, we would all be dead.

The waiters and waitresses were giving us dirty looks too, if the others keep this up, we would be booted out soon.

"Guys it's my birthday, I don't want to be chucked out on my birthday." I try to reason with them but I might as well have been talking to the wall.

Eamon is tucking into a plate of rabbit food, I think it is called a Caesar salad on the menu while grinning at the antics of the others, like chucking food around is the funniest joke ever. Me? I am just annoyed.

"Max, can I try one of your chips?" Eamon asks his hand already on Max's plate.

Max grabs Eamon's wrist, twisting it viciously. "I don't want your hand in my food, you queer son of a bitch."

"Max. You're hurting me," Eamon gasps.

"I will hurt you like I did before, you fucking queer."

Silence falls on the table like a ton of bricks. I am having trouble breathing. Eamon's whole body slumps. He bends his head, instantly I know he is moments away from tears.

I push my chair back, "Max, let go of my brother before I fucking hammer you."

Max is looking at Eamon with such hatred. I go towards Max and he lets go of Eamon's wrist. Eamon pulls back his arm, rubbing his wrist.

"Sorry Joe but I don't want your brother touching my food," says Max. Adding viciously, "God knows what I might catch."

I jump up towards Max to smash his head on the table but Eamon gets between us and bars my way. "Eamon fucking move," I order.

"Joe no, don't, he's not worth it, he's just a stupid bigot."

I barely hear my brother, I want to do my talking with my fists. If only Eamon would move out of the bloody way.

"Don't you ever talk to my brother like that again, do you fucking hear me! I owe you a fucking hammering for hitting him last time."

Max is on his feet, nostrils flaring now; if only my brother would get out of the way.

"If you gentlemen can't behave, then I must ask you to leave," says the manager who seems to appear from nowhere. Behind her are three of her waiters who look really pissed off and would like nothing better than to throw us out.

"Come on guys," says Max, pushing his plate of steak and chips away in disgust. "I've lost my appetite anyway, let's get out of this dump."

Max's lips are clamped together and his fist clenched at his side. But I am more than ready for him. But it is Luca who makes me pause, he is smiling, not laughing at me and Eamon and actually when I looked again, I realised he is smirking.

Then he gives a slight secret smile that is directed solely at Max. Rory is already on his feet. Luca is the last to stand. He and I exchange the look of mutual loathing as he heads out of the restaurant after Max and Rory.

Eamon sits back down at the table, his head bent. I place a hand on my brother's shoulder, he is shaking and trying his best to hide it.

Good riddance, I think as I watch the others swagger out. Until I realise they have stuck me with the damn bill.

Bastards.

38

Joey

"You should've let me punch his lights out," I am fuming at Eamon as we walk home.

The bill has wiped me out completely. Even with the money Dad had given me for a night out, being stuck with the bill for an extra three meals means I had to break out my plastic. My account is now empty.

But that is nothing compared to the rage I still feel at all the things Max has said to my brother. Even now I couldn't get Max's words out of my head. Eamon and I walk in silence, he hasn't said a word since leaving the bar, mind you I wasn't feeling too chatty myself.

Why had Max reacted so vilely to Eamon? God, I just need to get home. We are almost there, a couple of more minutes, I will be indoors. All I can think of now is Rosie, I just want to hold my daughter and try and make sense of the world in that order. I just want to—

Everything stopped.

Darkness. Then flashing lights behind my eyes and a searing pain in my head.

I find myself lying on the pavement, my head is pounding, there's a buzzing in my ears.

I try to stand up but I am knocked down again. My head is screaming with pain.

It takes a minute or two, to realise why I can't move. Someone is kneeling on my legs and my arms have been pulled back, I think, by someone else.

With great effort, I manage to lift my head but can't get my vision in focus.

I blink several times and my vision starts to become clear. I can see Max pushing Eamon backwards and hand slapping him on the face, Eamon keeps going backwards until his back is against the wall that makes up the side of a house.

But still Max keeps pushing, keeping him off balance.

"Max, stop it, leave him alone!" I yell as loud as possible.

Max just turns and laughs at me, this just makes Rory and Luca pull even harder on my arms. I feel something pop in my shoulder area and a fierce pain like an electric shock travels down my arm.

I feel my arm has come out of its socket and they are going to do the same to my other arm. But the pain in my arm is nothing compared to what is going on inside me as I watch Max and my brother.

He is punching Eamon and every time Eamon tries to straighten up, Max would punch him again. But that didn't stop my brother from trying to straighten up. And all the time, Eamon never takes his eyes off Max.

Every time Max punches him, he is saying things to him, "you're disgusting, you little fairy, you're a filthy little queer. You make my skin crawl," Max hisses.

Every word felt like a punch to my stomach. I flinch with every insult.

But Eamon doesn't say a word.

"Queer, shirt lifter, poff, faggot." Max goes through every derogatory name he can think of to chuck at my brother. And each name is followed with a punch. I can see blood pouring from my brother's face.

I don't know if I am roaring out loud or if it is just in my head, I feel like a savage beast. I've got to get free but can't loosen the grip they have on me for a second.

"Max, leave him alone, let him go, you fucking prick. Why don't you try me for size instead of someone smaller, you fucking knob."

And then Eamon does something that makes our world stop. He pushes Max, then grabs his face, leans in and kisses him on the lips.

Luca and Rory forget to yank at my arms, I forget to struggle, Max forgets to speak and I forget how to move. But only for a moment. Just a moment then all hell breaks loose.

Max totally loses it.

There is no other way to describe it, he roars out and grabs my brother, punching and punching my brother non-stop into the face.

Eamon puts his arms up to try and protect himself but it doesn't work. Max is beating the crap out of him.

Eamon falls to the ground, curling into a ball. But Max continues punching and now kicking him, with not even a pause between blows.

I struggle like a madman to free myself to help Eamon but I am still pinned down and they are now also punching me while I lie there, struggling and helpless.

Max is standing up right now, kicking my brother's head and stomping on it over and over and jumping on his arms.

"You always thought you were better than us, off to university," Luca hisses in my ear. "Truth is you're a lowlife paddy with a kid, no job and a queer for a brother."

I try everything to free myself, all I can do is turn my head and see Max and my brother. He is still beating Eamon, blood dripping off Max's fists and Eamon no longer moving.

All I have is words, so I try to entice him over to me.

"GET OFF HIM, MAX! ITS YOU WHO'S FUCKING QUEER, ALWAYS THOUGHT YOU WERE BENT AND IT WASN'T JUST ME WHO THOUGHT IT, WAS IT RORY?"

Rory jumps to his feet to kick me, Luca is rushing over to Max shouting, "Max stop, that's enough!" That gives me the opportunity and I jump up, my left fist ready. I can't move my right much but I am left-handed so I know I had a chance.

I punch Rory on the side of his head, he falls away grunting in pain. I hit him again pushing him to the ground and then I kick him a couple of times to make sure he stays down.

I jump on Max. I wrap my good arm round his neck and I drop him back so hard and fast that only his heels are touching the ground. I choke him just enough and then drop him without a second thought and then I run back to Eamon.

I kneel down beside my brother, he is lying on his side. I can't make out any of his features. His entire face is covered in blood.

"Eamon?" I whisper.

I put my fingers on his neck, to feel for a pulse.

"Max, we've got to get out of here, now!" Luca shouts at Max helping him up from the ground.

"WHAT'S GOING ON?" shouts a stocky man in pyjama bottoms and nothing else, "oh my God, call an ambulance Sara and call the police," he shouts over his shoulder.

Max is staring at me. "Brophy, you're a dead man."

I look up and get so close to Max, we are nearly touching noses. I look into his eyes. "You better fucking disappear. I'll go to prison for you," I speak the words quietly but I mean every single one of them.

Fist clenched, I wait; the only way any of them would get to Eamon again was over my dead body. The stocky man has made his way over and tries to take me away from Max, while telling the others to get away or he'd beat them and his wife has come out with a baseball bat and hands it to him.

"Max, come on you fucking idiot, let's go!" Lucas shouts. Rory and Luca take off, dragging Max behind them.

I drop to my knees. Eamon's face is such a mess of blood. I don't know what to do.

"Eamon?" I stroke his head and whisper, "Eamon, don't die, please don't die."

I could hear the distant noise of sirens getting closer, thank God.

39

Joey

I sit in the waiting room of the hospital which is half full but I feel totally alone and time moves so slowly.

Eamon is rushed through from the ambulance, thank God! But they wouldn't allow me to go through with him. I'm so scared, I say a prayer in my head begging God to save him.

I see two men walking through the doors and approach the reception desk, they speak to the receptionist who nods her head towards me.

One is a stocky white guy and the other a tall black guy. I stand up as they approach me.

"Are you the guy who came in with the victim of the assault?" asks tall black guy.

I nod.

"I'm Detective Sergeant Ray Johns, this is my colleague Detective Constable Adam Price, would you please tell us your name?"

"Joseph—Joe Brophy."

"So Joe, is it okay to call you Joe?"

"Yes," I reply quietly.

"Could you tell us what happened?" asks the sergeant, Constable Price has his pen poised over his notebook.

I just sit there in silence, I couldn't think where to start or what to say.

"Okay let's start with, do you know the name of the victim?"

"Yes, he's my brother Eamon Brophy. He's sixteen. No sorry, he turned seventeen a couple of weeks ago."

"Can you tell me what happened?" asks Sergeant Johns.

"We were jumped on the way home," I reply.

"Do you think you remember how many there were?"

"Three," I reply.

"Listen, you look a bit shaky, let's sit down and Constable Price can get you a hot drink."

I sit down and Sergeant John sits across from me, "I can see you are still in a state of shock, anything you can tell us will help us catch the ones who did this." Constable Price returns with a cup of tea, he puts it in front of me on the table.

"Take your time, just try and remember as much as possible."

I take a sip of the sweet hot tea.

"Eamon and I went out to—it's my birthday." Oh God, it's still my birthday.

I take another sip of the sickly tea, as my throat feels like it is closing up.

"Go on Joe," urges DS Johns.

"We were walking home and they jumped us at the top of our road," I reply.

"Did you recognise or know any of them?" asks DS Johns.

I pause, I don't know why. "Yes, I know all of them. Luca Peters, Rory Jackson and Max Matthews. Max was the one who beat Eamon to a pulp, while the others held me down. He just kept punching and kicking him, over and over, I tried—I did, I really tried to get free from the other two."

I put my head in my hands and feel tears and blood trickling down my face. "He just wouldn't stop," and I start to cry more.

"I'm sorry Joe but we have a few more questions to ask, are you okay to continue?"

"Yes." And the questions keep coming. I try to give them as much detail as possible; after around half an hour and by the time they leave, I am exhausted.

I find I can't stop shivering, I keep thinking back to the ambulance and the paramedics who had battled to clear Eamon's airways, his face was so distorted and swollen, they put a drip in his arm and an oxygen mask over his nose and mouth, they were battling to save Eamon's life.

And when they managed to stabilise him, we were put in the ambulance and blue lighted across the city. I didn't take my eyes off Eamon, I watched my brother lying unconscious praying silently, afraid I was going to lose him.

Once we got to the hospital, Eamon was whisked away to be x-rayed and operated on.

All of a sudden I think, crap I need to ring dad but I have no idea how to break this to him. The phone is answered after a couple of things.

"Hiya Joey, what's cutting? (That was the Irish way of asking what you are up to.)"

"I'm hoping you're on your way home guys, it's getting a bit late. Did you have a good time at least?" Dad's cheerful voice makes me want to burst into tears, I feel like a child. "And I hope you haven't been worrying about Rosie, she's fast asleep, went out like a light, she's such a good baby. Mind you, Eamon and yourself were good babies, don't know what's happened since," he says with a laugh.

"Dad, I'm at the hospital."

"WHAT? WHY? What's happened?" I could hear the change in his tone.

"Eamon, its Eamon. Eamon was beaten up, he's in a really bad way Dad, he was so badly beaten."

A male doctor who is built like a rugby player appears in front of me, I'm tall but I have to look up to this guy. "Joe, can you come with me, we need to check you over and you shouldn't really be using a mobile phone is this area."

"I'm just talking to my Dad."

"Okay, talk to him once I've made sure you're alright," the doctor insists.

"Okay."

I don't know if Dad heard the doctor talk to me or maybe it is just the sound of my voice, as I was feeling so scared for myself. Either way, Dad didn't hang around.

"I'm on my way," and he hangs up.

"I don't need to be examined, I want to stay with my brother," I insist as I put my phone back into my trouser pocket.

"He's in very good hands," the doctor tries to reassure me. "He's in theatre but in the meantime, we need to check you over, you're bleeding from your head and your shoulder looks like it's either broken or dislocated."

I had minor cuts and grazes and severe bruising down my back, my legs. I didn't hurt too much though. I also had cuts to my left knuckles and also stitches in my head and a minor cut to my face which also had stitches.

My shoulder was indeed dislocated and terribly painful when they popped it back in but I am getting gas and air which helped a bit. I am now sitting here in a sling and I have been given painkillers thankfully, so the pain in my shoulder has lessened.

Dad arrives at the hospital within 30 minutes after I had come out from having stitches, he is carrying a sleeping Rosie. The moment I see her, I reach out to take her. "No it's okay," says Dad, "I've got her. No point waking her up and I don't think you will be able to hold her properly with that sling, is it broken Joey?"

I don't answer Dad as I am away somewhere else in my mind. The three of us sit in the waiting area in intense silence. I've done more praying in the last hours than I've ever done in my life. Eamon could've died, he still could.

I couldn't imagine life without him, we are so close. We continue to sit in the silence with Rosie fast asleep in Dad's arms. Eventually Dad asks the question I've been dreading.

"What happened?" Dad asks at last. I am so lost in my own thoughts that when he spoke it made me jump.

"We got attacked," I reply.

"By who?"

"By some guys from my old school," I say.

"What, these are guy's you knew?" Dad asks.

"Yes," I reply but I tell him who and what has happened; before he could answer, the doors to the hospital open and Auntie Mary is running in. She runs up and hugs Dad and me. Dad explains briefly to Auntie Mary what has happened and tells her Eamon is in theatre right now.

Auntie Mary is hugging me again, "jaysus Joey, are you okay?"

Dad looks at me and says, "Why didn't you stop them, why didn't you protect your brother?"

"Dad, I tried, they held me down while Max just kept beating Eamon, until I got free of them." I start to cry quietly, my head in my hands.

"Jack stop," cries Auntie Mary, "don't you know Joe would do everything in his power to protect Eamon?"

"Keep out of this Mary, it's my son who is fighting for his life in there," answers Dad.

"And you have a son who's sitting next to you who could do with a kind word," says Auntie Mary.

I stand up, I can't listen to this. "Excuse me."

"Where are you going?" Dad asks.

I have to get out of there. "I need the loo." I head for the men's room before Dad or Auntie Mary could say another word. No matter how much Dad blames me, it couldn't compare with how much I blamed myself. But his words still hurt.

I wash my face, I look at myself in the mirror. I have a few cuts on my face including the one they stitched, I also have quite a few stitches in my head but nothing in comparison to what Eamon is going through. And this is all my fault.

I head back to the waiting area but before I turn the corner to go in I could hear my Auntie Mary talking to Dad.

"I'm just saying you've always been too hard on that boy, you're blaming him for things that's not his fault," says Auntie Mary.

"You haven't a clue what you're talking about," Dad dismisses.

I didn't turn the corner to enter the waiting area. Mary and Dad are talking about me, so I stop and listen.

"Oh, so you don't think I haven't a clue, you think me and my sister didn't talk? Do you think she didn't confide in me?" My aunt challenges. "She told me she knew how much you resented her and Joey for what happened."

"Rubbish, I didn't resent her. I married her, didn't I?" says Dad.

"But you didn't want to at first, did you? And you made sure Annie knew that."

"I was young and scared, Mary but I did the right thing," says Dad.

"Oh yes, you did the right thing in the end," says Mary.

"Mary, give me a break. I was only 19, for God sake; it wasn't an ideal way to start a marriage."

"The only reason you married Annie was because she was pregnant with Joey, do you think she didn't know how much you resented her and your son? She knew you didn't love her."

"That's a damn lie. When Annie died, I wanted to die too. Only two things got me out of bed each morning, Joey and Eamon."

"My sister loved you so much and all she wanted was for you to love her back."

"What the hell are you talking about, Mary?" Dad shouts. "I loved her, she was my whole life."

"Then why did you never tell her that Jack, you never told her you loved her," says Auntie Mary.

Dad replies so quietly I have to strain to hear him. "Annie knew that I loved her. I didn't have to tell her, she knew I was never kind of good with those words."

"The same way your boys know it?" asks Auntie Mary. "When do you show Joey you love him, every time you put him down? The way you show Eamon you love him by not even acknowledging the fact that he's gay? Is that how your boys know it?"

"Of course I know he's gay. I've come to terms with that," says Dad angrily. "Don't make me out to be the bad person Mary, just because I don't talk about it every two seconds."

"No one's asking you to talk about it every two seconds, Jack but you won't talk about it at all."

Deep silence, then Auntie Mary speaks, "Jack I'm not here to argue with you, this is neither the time nor the place."

"I'm glad you finally realise that," says Dad, "nice to see your opinion of me hasn't changed one bit from the day I married your sister."

"That's not true," says Auntie Mary. "All I ever wanted was what was best for you, my sister and my nephews."

"Don't you think that's what I want too?"

"Then why didn't you tell Joey the truth about—?"

I walk round the corner. Auntie Mary stops talking. Dad and my aunt both stare at me. Each of us knows I'd heard every word. But knowing the truth hurt even worse.

"You only married mum because she was pregnant with me," I whisper. "All this time, all these years, I wondered why you never looked at me or treated me the same as Eamon."

The answer is simple. Eamon was wanted. I wasn't. And now everything seems to make sense, the way Dad reacted to my A-level results. And his comment, 'if I had your chances I'll be a millionaire by now'.

"That's why nothing I ever did was good enough." I realised I've just spoken aloud. "You blame me for ruining your life, for stopping you from doing all the things you wanted to do."

Dad hands Rosie to Auntie Mary and comes over to me, "listen to me, Joey. You are wrong," he says. "Yes, your mum and I probably wouldn't have married if she hadn't been pregnant with you but I cared very much about you and your mum and I still do."

"That's why nothing I ever did was good enough, you blamed me for ruining your life. And stopping you doing all the things you wanted to do."

"Joey listen, if I made you feel like that then I'm sorry, it was never my intention. If I pushed you too hard, it's because I didn't want you to make my mistakes."

"Yeah, I was your biggest mistake, wasn't I?" I try to pull away but Dad grabs me and turns me round.

"No, Joey, you weren't," Dad insists. "Sometimes the thing you're convinced that you don't want turns out to be the best thing ever, I'm guessing you know what I mean as you have Rosie and how you feel now about her in contrast to when she first arrived.

"My family is the only thing that's ever been important to me and that has never changed. And yeah, I had plans before your mum got pregnant, I was going to finish university, I was going to be an architect but if I could live my life all over again, I wouldn't change anything except your mother passing away too soon.

"Not one single thing, do you understand? Do you believe me, Joey? It's really important that you believe me."

"Mr Brophy?" The surgeon appears still in his scrubs. Both my Dad and I freeze.

Dad manages to pull himself together, steps forward and says, "how is Eamon, is he okay?"

I'm still standing in the same spot. I can't seem to move, I just keep repeating in my head, please God let him be okay, please God let him be okay. The surgeon then starts to speak.

"Eamon sustained a number of serious injuries, his eye socket was shattered, his jaw and nose are broken, he also has three broken ribs and a broken ankle and wrist, he also has numerous cuts and bruises over most of his body but he's out of theatre and he's stable."

"Can we see?" Dad asks.

"Just for a moment but I have to warn you, his face is going to take a long time to heal and he may have a couple of permanent scars, also I need to prepare you for what you are going to see as we had to wire his jaw, realign his nasal bone and the surrounding tissue and we had to use metal plates and screws to hold his right cheek bone in place. I just need you to understand at present Eamon is on a ventilator to help with his breathing."

I take Rosie from my Auntie Mary and rest her head on my shoulder, she barely stirred still fast asleep, we followed the surgeon.

"Oh my god," Dad whispers.

"Holy Mary, mother of God," gasps Auntie Mary grabbing her throat.

The surgeon tried to prepare us but this is far worse than we could've ever imagined. All I can do is stare, I want to turn away but can't. His face is more swollen and distorted than before; there is nothing about his face that I recognised.

He has bandages wrapped around his head and jaw and under his chin; an oxygen mask over his mouth and nose, he has a drip of colourless solution running into one arm and a bag of blood running into the other and a monitor that keeps beeping with lines and numbers on it.

The surgeon is speaking and my brain tunes back in, "our concern is his breathing," the surgeon tells us. "Eamon suffered displaced rib fractures and what with that and his facial injuries, we have to monitor his breathing very carefully. And we managed to save his right eye but he's not out of the woods by a long shot."

Auntie Mary starts to cry quietly next to me, she tries to control it but fails.

Dad puts his arm around Auntie Mary trying to comfort her and he is gulping like a fish out of water.

The surgeon continues, "Eamon is young and strong and with time, there is no reason why he shouldn't make an excellent recovery," the surgeon is trying to reassure us.

As I look at Eamon, the only thought that comes into my head is that Max is going to pay for this, going to pay big time. My beautiful brother, I brush away my tears with the back of my hand; yes, he is going to pay.

40

Vinnie

We all follow the surgeon from the room and back out into the waiting room, the surgeon says, "needless to say the next 24 hours is crucial and he will be constantly monitored."

"I'm going to stay with him, is that okay doctor?" asks my father.

"Yes of course, I will get a couple of chairs put in there for you," replies the surgeon.

Dad shakes his hand and thanks him for saving his son's life.

"Your son's life was saved by the paramedics that attended the scene, I'm just putting the pieces back together," replies the surgeon.

Nevertheless, we all know that the surgeon is under playing his part. He says goodbye to us and continues back to theatre to help the next poor devil, I suppose.

I look around and realise that dawn is breaking and Rosie is still sleeping soundly which is amazing.

Dad turns to me and says, "Joey, you go home with Auntie Mary."

"No, Dad. I want to stay with you and sit with Eamon."

"Listen Joey, you've got Rosie to think of, if you can get her settled, maybe Auntie Mary would stay with her and then you can come back to the hospital."

"No need to ask Jack, of course I'll stay with Rosie," replies Auntie Mary.

This is fine by me as Rosie has really taken to Auntie Mary and this allows me to go back and sit with my brother.

All of a sudden, we hear someone running through the doors to the reception area and we are surprised to see its Vinny O'Brien, he doesn't seem to notice us standing there and he rushes over to the reception and is asking about Eamon.

The receptionist is pointing to us.

"Why is Vincent O'Brien here?" Dad asks.

"Not a clue, Dad."

Vinnie comes over and shakes Dad's hand, "I'm sorry Mr Brophy. I heard what happened, well I heard Eamon was beaten up." Vinny turns to me, "who did this, Joey? I'm telling you now I'm going to make them pay for this."

"Vincent, stop!" says Dad.

"Look Vinnie, we have more than enough going on, the police have been informed and are dealing with it and can I ask as nice as it is for you to show so much concern, why?"

Vinnie looks at Dad, then looks at me and seems to take a deep breath.

"Ahh. Well, we are kind of seeing each other, Eamon wanted to tell you but I asked him not to until I told my family about my sexuality, which I have now done. Eamon is an amazing person who helped me come to terms with who I am and I'm not hiding who I am anymore."

Gobsmacked is an underestimation of mine and Dad's faces and Auntie Mary is the 1st to recover. "I'm so pleased you've got each other and I guessing you'd like to see Eamon, is that okay with you, Jack?" asks Auntie Mary.

"Er. Yes, yes but Vinny I need to warn you, you probably won't even recognise him, he's that badly beaten," Dad replies.

We say good night and I hug Dad goodbye as did Auntie Mary who hugs Vinny also and we watch them heading to Eamon's room. And I and Auntie Mary head for home.

As they walk into Eamon's room, Dad watches the reaction on Vincent's face, it is a look of pure shock and horror. "Sweet Jesus, my God!" exclaims Vinnie, he then rushes over and takes Eamon's hand. "Eamon, it's Vinny I'm here. Mr Brophy, who did this to him, I need to know."

"Listen Vinny, I will tell you but you must not go after them, as this will only get you in trouble and it won't help Eamon. I understand how you feel and yes, Joey and I would love to go out and smash the fuck out of Max, Rory and Luca.

"We're not going down that route, not going down to their level so I want you to promise as I also made Joey promise, let the police deal with it. And Vinny call me Jack, Mr Brophy makes me feel ancient."

"So it was those fuckers, I can't believe they would do this. I'd say Max is the ringleader to this attack but I'm telling you now Jack, if the police don't get them, I will and that is a promise."

"It was Max that hammered Eamon and Luca and Rory held Joey down, dislocated his shoulder," says Jack.

"But why Jack, what made them do this?" as Vincent looked at Eamon with tears in his eyes.

"For being gay," Dad provides, his voice bitter. "I thought this gay bashing bullshit was a thing of the past or at least it's supposed to be."

"Jesus Christ, I can't believe that, why wasn't I there to protect him; this wouldn't have happened if I was there," says Vincent sadly.

"Jesus had nothing to do this, Vincent," says Dad harshly. "Just homophobic dirt bags who didn't even have the guts to make it a fair fight."

"Well, I tell you now Jack, if the police let them away, this I swear on my life; I'll make it a fair fight just me and my old man's Hurley and I'll take the three of them out," Vincent says angrily.

And Jack believed him, praying the police dealt with them instead of Vincent O'Brien.

41

Joey

Eamon is doing pretty well, after two days he is off the ventilator and has moved from ICU to side room on a normal ward. We all spend a lot of time at the hospital but it is Dad and Vinnie who stayed with him during his critical time.

And they both seem to get on like a house on fire, bonding over both their love for Eamon.

It's now Eamon's fifth day and myself, Dad and Rosie arrive at the ward and go to my brother's room to find his bed empty.

Dad sprints to the nurse's station, closely followed by me and Rosie in her buggy, the same fear gripping both of us.

"Where's my son? Eamon Brophy?" Dad demands of the male nurse.

"Oh Mr Brophy, I'm sorry, I meant to catch you before you got to his room, can you come with me please?"

"Where is my son?" Dad asks again, his voice a whisper. Eamon.

All of a sudden I feel so cold. I feel like my blood has frozen inside me.

Don't think the worst.

Don't think. Just wait.

The nurse leads the way back to Eamon's room. "Mr Brophy, we had to take Eamon back to theatre," he says. "A scan revealed a nasal septal hematoma, which was causing a blockage in his breathing. So he's been taken back to theatre to have the haematoma drained."

Dad sits down in the nearest chair, "oh God."

"Is he going to be okay? Is he going to make it?" I ask.

"Don't say that Joey, of course he'll be okay," Dad replies.

"Your son is lucky, he was in the right place at the right time, so he's been dealt with straightaway and draining a haematoma is actually quite a straightforward procedure," says the nurse. "So don't worry, he's in the best hands and if you wait here, he should be back from Theatre very soon."

"Thank you," says Dad.

I and Dad sit there, me pushing Rosie back and forth in her buggy. Next thing, the door opens and in walks Vinny with a coffee.

"Oh sorry guys, I went out to call you and let you know about Eamon and then went to get a coffee, needless to say I've got your voicemail and I did try your mobile as well, Joey but the same, it went to voicemail.

"I would've gotten you a coffee if I'd known you were here, would you like me to go and get you a couple now?"

"Thanks Vinny, I switched my mobile ringer off when I got into the hospital, so I missed your call, were you here when they took him down to theatre? And what happened exactly?" I ask still pushing Rosie backwards and forwards in her buggy.

"Well, he was having a bit of trouble breathing, so I called the nurse and she put an oxygen mask on him and called the doctor and then he was taken straight away for a scan and straight to theatre after that, they told me he would be fine, that it was caught very quickly so the haematoma hadn't got very big."

"Thanks Vinny, I'm glad you were here with him, that he wasn't on his own," says Dad.

"No problem Jack, sure where else would I be," replies Vinnie.

Rosie is getting restless and wants out of the buggy. I unclip the safety harness and sit her on my knee but she still wouldn't settle.

"Dad, can you hold Rosie for a second?" I hand Rosie over then look in the baby bag and lift out her favourite rabbit and also her favourite book which is all chewed around the corners.

I hold them out to her and say, "Which one Rosie?" Rosie reaches for her rabbit. She drops it on the floor by accident and Vinny reaches down and retrieves it for her, he starts to play peekaboo with the rabbit and Rosie, which makes Rosie squeal with laughter.

We all sit there in silence, apart from Vinny who is playing with Rosie.

Rosie is now toddling across the floor to Vinny then running back to me.

Next thing I know, there is a terrific smell, of course it's Rosie.

"It seems Rosie needs changing," I say. "I'll just nip to the baby changing room." I grab the baby bag and Rosie and head off.

I change Rosie but also realise that I haven't packed any extra nappies so that one I just put on her is the last one. So I need to nip out and get some nappies and luckily the hospital isn't far from the High Street.

I go back to the room and Eamon isn't back yet.

"Dad, I forgot to pack Rosie's nappies and I've used the only one I had with me, so I'm going to nip down to the baby shop on the High Street just to get some more nappies. I won't be long, will you look after Rosie till I get back please?"

"That's no problem Joey, you nip off. I've got Rosie no problem," replies Dad.

So off I go to the High Street and into the baby shop. It seems funny this is the first time I've actually been into the baby shop as it seems that Dad got everything for Rosie in the beginning and now I realise how much money Dad actually laid out; the prices are horrendous for buggies, cots, highchairs, etc.

I find the nappies and I buy extra baby wipes and pay at the till and leave the shop. As I leave the shop, I can't believe my eyes; across the road is Luca, walking along not a care in the world.

He hasn't seen me so I have the advantage, I cross the road and I am then walking behind him but he still hasn't seen me, just as he walks past an alleyway, I grab him and push him into the alleyway.

"Where the fuck is he, Luca?" I ask pushing him hard against the wall.

"Who, Joey?" says Luca.

"Don't try and be smart Luca, where the fuck is Max?" as I bang his head against the wall.

"I don't know, I swear I don't know, let me go." As he struggles to get away from me.

The police haven't been able to find Max or Rory for that matter, the only one they have interviewed is Luca.

"Why Luca? We used to be friends, why would you want to hurt me and Eamon? Max nearly killed Eamon, at this very moment, he's in theatre all because of you lot."

"What! He shouldn't be so fucking gay then," he says laughing.

I grab him by the neck and start to choke him. I have totally lost the plot. I keep squeezing and squeezing and Lucas' face gets redder and redder. His eyes start to bulge, I don't care. I want him dead.

Then someone grabs me from behind and pulls me off and Luca falls to the floor, gasping like a fish. I swing around expecting to see either Rory or Max or both but it is Vinnie.

"Joey, this isn't the way and don't forget we made a promise to your Dad," Vinny says holding my head and looking into my face. I nod my head and then sink to the floor as the adrenaline leaves my body. I watch as Vinny goes over to Luca and lifts him clean off the floor.

"Well now Luca, I think young Joey here was asking you a question, so shall we try again? Get your breath back and start talking before I break you in half. Where are Max and Rory?" Vinnie snarls.

Vinny slams his hand right next to Luca's head hitting the wall, "Now Luca, I'm not mucking about, the next time it will be your head so I'll ask the question again; where are they?"

"Okay Vinny, they are staying with Rory's uncle but I don't know the address."

"What's the uncle's name? And what area does he live in?" asks Vinny.

Luca looks at Vinny and says, "His uncle's name is Mark Slark and they live outside of the town, I think it's a small holding."

"See now Luca that wasn't too difficult was it, now there is one other thing."

And with that he punches Luca straight into the mouth, "that one's for Eamon and be glad I didn't put my full force behind it." As the blood spurts out from Lucas' mouth.

Vinny leans down and puts his hand out to me and pulls me up, "come on Joey, let's get back to the hospital."

"Oh and by the way Luca, don't go warning them because on your head be it, it's you I will come after." And with that Vinny and I leave.

On the walk back to the hospital, I ring Detective Johns and give him the information that Luca has given to us, he says he will be able to find Rory's uncle and thanks us for the information and it would be dealt with as soon as possible.

We arrive back at the hospital to find Rosie asleep in Dad's arms and Eamon asleep in his bed, it is a relief to see Eamon back and breathing on his own.

Dad says Eamon has only just got back to his room and that his operation has gone well.

We all sit down and wait for Eamon and Rosie to wake up.

42

Joey

4 Months Later

Eamon is home now, he's still recovering but he's coming on really well. I think a lot of this is to do with Vinny, he's been a great support for him but he doesn't smile anymore; he's lost his sparkle.

Tonight I am so tired, I've not been getting a lot of sleep due to Rosie's teeth playing her up, I tiptoe into my bedroom trying not to wake her but it's like she has built-in radar and she just seems to know when I come in to the room and straight away, she starts to stir and just as I nearly reach my bed, she pulls herself up and is looking at me.

"Back to sleep, Rosie," and I try to get her to lie down but nope, she's having none of it. Rosie holds out her arms and wiggles her fingers at me to pick her up.

So of course I give in, I sit down on the bed with pillows propping me up with Rosie resting her head on my shoulder, she's so content.

"Dada," says Rosie.

"What did you say, Rosie?" I whisper.

"Dada," she repeats.

"Who is Dada?" I ask.

She presses her little finger against my cheek and says, "Dada."

I jump up with Rosie taking her into Dad's room, "Dad, Dad!"

Dad sits up quickly blinking his eyes, his eyes still looking glazed, "what's wrong, is something wrong with Rosie?"

"Listen to this Dad, say it Rosie."

Rosie says nothing and Dad is looking at me like I've lost my mind, so I try again.

"Rosie, who am I?" I say pointing at myself. "Tell Grandad," I coax.

"Dada," Rosie says giggling and I laugh too.

Then she says it again, "dada." I spin her around lifting her high above my head, she is giggling and so am I.

"Did you hear that, Dad? She said Dada."

"That's great, well done Rosie, now feck off Joey, its 1 o'clock in the morning and I have to be up for work soon," says Dad, falling back into his pillows and closing his eyes.

I smile and say, "Dad, you have to watch your language now with Rosie starting to talk." With that he throws a pillow at me, which misses but seems to amuse Rosie who bursts out giggling.

I look at Dad and from the light from the landing, I can see his face, eyes shut, smiling. "Night Dad," I say as I take Rosie back to our room and put her in the cot. I say, "Night Rosie, go to sleep now, daddy loves you very much."

And I get into bed wondering what Dad had mumbled as we left his room, it sounded like, "Love you son." But maybe its wishful thinking.

43
Joey

Court

Well, after a week of being in court and standing up in front of everyone, telling what happened that awful night was hard, I can't even imagine how hard it was for Eamon to relive that night in court in front of the three people who had inflicted that beating on him.

I usually take Rosie everywhere with me but not to court. Aunty Mary is looking after her. Today is the sentencing as they have all been found guilty and Rory and Max are already remanded in custody but not Luca.

The results are in. Max received six years with no remission, Rory received eighteen months for his part in the attack and Luca because he helped the police with their enquiries into finding Max and Rory, received four months.

We were also glad to be able to thank the man and his wife who had come out of their house that night and stopped the attack and called the ambulance for Eamon, as he also had to give evidence.

We all shook his hand and thanked him but Dad was very emotional, hugging him and his wife, thanking them for saving his son's life. And at last it's a chapter in our lives that we can close and now repair ourselves mentally to get over it.

It is all finished by early afternoon and we leave the court to head home, the cold air hits us but it is nearly Christmas, Dad thinks it's going to snow. I feel exhausted and starving by the time we get home.

Auntie Mary hugs us all, she knows the outcome of the court case as Dad had phoned her. She says, "I've left sandwiches and soup in the kitchen, the soup just needs heating, now I'm afraid I've got to go as I have an appointment."

Walking towards the door, getting her coat on and waving goodbye to us all. Dad goes upstairs for a quick shower and Eamon goes upstairs to get changed.

I walk towards the kitchen to heat the soup for us all and get some pills as I have a banging headache, with Rosie following behind me. She keeps putting her arms up to me and saying park.

"Not today Rosie, no park today."

She starts to cry, "Daddy, park."

"No Rosie, not today, daddy is tired."

But Rosie doesn't give in, "park, park, park, park," she demands bursting into tears.

"No Rosie, not today, be a good girl for daddy." That is it. Rosie starts howling like a banshee, her wailing going straight through my head.

I couldn't take any more after the day I've just had.

"ROSIE, FOR GOD'S SAKE, SHUT UP."

She stops crying and stares at me for a stunned moment, then she really lets rip. If I thought she was loud before, it is nothing compared to what is coming out of her mouth now.

She is really doing my head in. I glare down at her, my fists slowly clenching. I am less than a second away from losing it.

So I run out of the kitchen into the sitting room, throwing myself down on the armchair. I bury my head in my hands, appalled at myself. I can't believe what I've almost done. Rosie's crying is getting closer. She peeps her head round the door still sobbing, looking at me with an uncertainty that twists my guts.

"I'm so sorry, Rosie." And I open my arms. Rosie runs to me and I scoop her up. Her sobbing is subsiding now as I hold her tight.

"Sorry, daddy."

"You've got nothing to be sorry about," I tell her, "I'm sorry I shouted at you. I love you, Rosie."

"Kiss, daddy?"

I nearly cry, I have to take a couple of gulps to hold down my tears, before I can speak, "Yes please Rosie," I whisper.

Rosie kisses me on the cheek. And I kiss her and all the time I'm thinking this is just like what Amy had told me in the beginning when she said she was losing it with Rosie and at that time I couldn't understand but I do now.

44

Eamon

I've only seen my face once in the mirror and I am so horrified by the large scar that I haven't looked in a mirror since. The surgeon says it will fade and I have cream to put on it which I do.

For some reason, Vinny doesn't seem to notice it; the same with little Rosie who strokes my face frequently and says, "Poor unckey." I thought I would feel, I don't know MORE after the court case, like a kind of relief but I don't, I still move around with the fear of being attacked.

All the family have been great making sure I'm okay. Christmas won't be long now. I can't wait to see Rosie on Christmas morning opening her presents. I just love her so much, she has made our family into a proper family. No matter how sad I'm feeling, Rosie just makes me smile and her laugh is infectious.

The first time ever today I heard Joey shout at Rosie, I was going to go downstairs and confront him but I just sat on the stairs and listened and heard him so upset and apologising to her.

I think the problem is we are all exhausted mentally and physically and emotionally, Joey is lucky that Dad was in the shower and didn't hear him shouting at Rosie because he would've gone mental.

Vinnie is working late a lot, at the moment he's converting some old warehouses into studios but he still makes time for me.

My friends, Roxanne, Lizzie, Ruby, Dylan and Zach are constantly calling me to make sure I am okay and they want to come round and see me. But I can't face anybody, not yet; maybe in a little while when I get used to my face.

Also it seems I'm going to receive some victim compensation and the amount they are saying is £85,000 and Joey doesn't know yet but he will also be receiving some money.

I think it's going to be round about £7000 which will really help him out, as he can't find a job to fit around Rosie. And I'm still getting these terrible headaches. I just wish they would go away.

45

Joey

Rosie adores the Christmas tree and wants the twinkly lights on all the time.

I try to explain Santa to Rosie. I'm not sure if she understands. I'm going to take her to see Father Christmas in town this afternoon, Dad said that she might be frightened of him as Eamon didn't like him when he was little.

Dad's at work and Eamon has gone to his victim support and is meeting Vinny after. Rosie toddles up to me. "Hungry, daddy," she tells me.

I smile at Rosie, "well then, let's get you something yummy to eat."

I take her hand and lead her into the kitchen. I put Rosie in her highchair, I put some banana slices in a bowl and place it in front of her and one of her favourite yoghurts. I stand and watch as she tucks in; using her spoon like a weapon, she attacks a banana slice.

I fill her drinking cup with warm milk, just as the doorbell rings. "Daddy won't be a moment, Rosie." I open the door to Auntie Mary.

"How it's cutting Joey, where's my favourite wee girl?"

"In the kitchen, Mary." Mary hugs me and rushes past me to get to the kitchen.

She walks in and Rosie looks up and says, "Mary."

"Did you hear that Joey? Rosie said Mary, jaysus Joey this one's as bright as a button," she says kissing Rosie on both cheeks.

"I'm off into town Joey and wondered if there's anything I can pick up for you to save you taking this hunny out in the cold."

"It's okay, Mary. I'm taking Rosie to see Santa this afternoon. So if you don't wanna go into town, I can pick stuff up for you."

"Well, what about this for an idea Joey, why don't we go together, that's if you don't mind an old lady tagging along with you?"

"No problem, Mary and if you get tired, we can get Rosie out of the buggy and put you in."

Auntie Mary laughs, saying, "cheeky bugger, if you don't watch yourself, I might put you in the buggy." She holds her fists up like a boxer. Which makes both me and Rosie laugh.

I get Rosie out of the highchair as she's finished her lunch and I start to pack her baby bag and put together some snacks for her to take with us to go into town; while Auntie Mary is entertaining Rosie, the doorbell goes.

"Dingdong," says Rosie. Auntie Mary goes to the door and I can hear her talking to someone and telling them to come in. I come out of the kitchen to see who it is and shock, horror it's Diane, the fucking social worker.

"Hello Joey, hello Rosie," says Diane as Rosie peeks out from behind my legs.

My Auntie Mary steps forward and holds out her hand to be shaken. "I am Joey's aunt, Mary Rooney," she says shaking Diane's hand.

"You got my message then about today's visit?" says Diane.

"Actually no, I didn't and I've made plans to take Rosie out this afternoon," I reply.

"Oh, well I left a voice message on your landline yesterday, well not to worry I'm here now and I'll try not to hold you up too long."

"So this is an official visit to discuss Rosie's future," Diane explains. "I was expecting your father to be here."

Quick as a fox Mary jumps in, "actually Jack, Joey's father had an appointment he couldn't get out of and asked me to step in and obviously, he forgot to mention it to Joey." Good old Auntie Mary covering our backsides.

Auntie Mary escorts Diane into the sitting room. "Will you take a cup of tea?" asks Mary.

"No thanks I'm fine, I would rather get started, so have you now got Rosie's red medical book," she says with her fake smile.

"No problem, here it is," I say and I exchange Diane's smile with one of my own equally as false.

I have made sure that the book is up-to-date so I was happy to hand it over. I had all my daughter's vaccinations in there and any other medical information that anyone would need. The polite conversation that follows is interlaced with questions.

She asks if I am collecting child benefit for Rosie. I wasn't. I assumed that wherever Amy is, she is getting that money. To my surprise, Diane tells me what steps I need to take to make sure that I've got Rosie's child benefit money instead of Amy.

And she also gives me advice about getting my name on Rosie's birth certificate; that way, I'll get full parental responsibilities and rights under the law and to try and get it all done before Rosie is two, otherwise it gets complicated.

I keep waiting for the tripwires but none appear. The whole thing takes close to an hour. And then she says, "I nearly forgot to ask, is she talking yet?"

Before I can answer, Auntie Mary is straight in there, "is she talking? She knows that many words, now she's like a little dictionary. She could talk the hind legs off a donkey." And then a strange thing happens. Diane starts to laugh which makes Rosie laugh and of course, when Rosie laughs we all laugh.

Then Rosie says pointing, "Daddy, Mary, Lady."

"Gosh, she's a bright little girl," says Diane.

"And she's not even two yet," I say unable keep the pride out of my voice as I bend down to kiss Rosie, stroking her hair, I tell her what a good girl she is.

"She means a lot to you, doesn't she?" Diane smiles genuinely.

"Yes, she does, she's my world." Diane then makes some notes and packs her bag, Mary retrieves Diane's coat for her and scarf and leads her to the front door saying goodbye to us all.

"Now Joey what were you talking about, that Diane is a very pleasant young lady and I think she helped you, at least now you can apply for your family allowance and get your name on the birth certificate, two things we didn't think about," says Auntie Mary.

"Right said Mary, we better get a shift on if Rosie is going to see Santa." I go to collect Rosie's coat, hat, scarf and gloves, boots and get her ready to go.

The three of us head out into the cold and before long, we are at the department store where Santa is making his appearance. We join a small queue and pay our money to an elf, who Rosie finds amusing.

Soon it's our turn and the three of us enter Santa's grotto. Auntie Mary insisted on coming with us and we don't mind because we both love her. Well, Rosie didn't like Santa, she cried at him and didn't want to take the present he was offering; maybe she's still a bit young but Mary, she loved Santa, in fact she's meeting him for lunch tomorrow and so Mary got a present from Santa as well.

46
Dad

Jaysus, what an eejit I am. I forgot to tell Joey about the social worker and I should have been there but it seems to have turned out okay, in fact she's given him some good advice.

And it seems Santa didn't go very well for Rosie but very well for Mary.

I'm glad Mary is meeting someone; she deserves it, she is truly an amazing woman who has helped me and the lads so much, when Annie died I felt like I was drowning with the responsibilities of the boys, the mortgage, bills, trying to work but Mary was my life jacket, my buoy, she kept us all afloat and now she's doing it again with Joey and Rosie.

I'm still worried about Eamon, he won't see any of his close friends but at least he has Vinny who has turned out to be a wonderful support to Eamon and a real strong person not just physically, mentally as well.

Vinny's parent's May and Padre have been great, sending round potatoes grown in their garden and home-made soda bread and home-made jam and meals.

And now at least the court case is over and those fuckers have got what they deserved, so I hope now we can all move on. It's going to be hard as I worry every time Joey or Eamon go out.

47

Vincent

Five days before Christmas and Vinnie comes round all excited.

"Joey, I think I found the answer to getting you a job. As you know, my mum is well-known for her great soda bread and also the scones, pickles and jams and potato cakes, well she's going to teach me and you to make all of these things and we are going to sell them in the Irish club.

"And as you know, we have such a large Irish community around here but nowhere to buy Irish produce but here's the shocker, we have two days as we're selling on Saturday, any questions," he says laughing.

"Yeah, I've got one," says Eamon, "what about me?"

"What do you mean?" asks Vinny. "I thought you wouldn't want to be involved as you don't really wanna see anybody at the moment."

"Yeah you're right Vinny but I'm quite happy to help on the cooking side."

"No problem Eamon, you're in, the more the merrier," replies Vinny.

"Well, it looks like we're all cooking for the next few days and I think you could be onto something here Vinny, like you said no one is providing this service for the Irish community," says Joey.

"Well, we'll start tonight; if you come round to my house in a couple of hours, Mum will be ready to start teaching us all her tricks, would your Dad be alright to have Rosie for a couple of hours?

"If not, you can bring her around; there's more than enough people in my house to entertain her. Is that okay with both of you?"

I and Eamon nod. "That's great," says Vinny. "I'll see you in a couple of hours."

48

Joey

We all pitched in with making all the produce; the soda bread, the potato cakes, scones and luckily enough, Vinny's mum had a surplus of pickles and jam that she gave us, so we didn't have to make them. To be fair though, I think Eamon and Vinny done far better than me making the bread.

Vinny's two younger sisters have put flyers through people's doors to advertise our sale in the Irish club on Saturday.

And when Saturday comes around, we are just about ready. Dad is looking after Rosie so off I went with Vinny to the Irish club.

By the time we set up the tables with our produce, we could see a small queue forming, so we at least know we are going to sell some stuff.

By 3 o'clock, we are totally sold out. I just couldn't believe it. And when we count up the money we have taken, £385 and a few odd pence, so taking into account we started selling at 1.30, that is amazing.

All the money is going back to Vinny's mum as she provides all the ingredients and the time, she tries to argue with us that she doesn't want the money but we insist because without her, we couldn't have done it.

"Vinny you are totally right, there is a market, a big market for Irish produce."

"Well Joey, I think this could be the start of something big so you better buckle up because I have a few ideas where I want to take this and myself and Eamon want you with us all the way."

49

Christmas Day

Well, it's Christmas day and snow is just fluttering down gently and I'm not sure that Rosie knows exactly what's going on but she's so excited, I think she is going to explode.

All the glittery presents under the tree are enticing Rosie to open them but she's also interested in the chocolates hanging on the branches of the tree, which are little animals and now the snow; well, she's fit to burst.

Auntie Mary is here helping Dad with the dinner and its great how they seem to be getting on so much better. I think they cleared the air in the hospital.

I call out. "Dad, Auntie Mary, can you come into the sitting room? We're gonna start opening the presents as Rosie can't wait any longer and neither can Eamon."

We all sit down, Eamon and Rosie on the floor, Eamon passing the presents out from under the tree. Rosie receives so many toys, she doesn't know what to play with first; so in true Rosie form, she sits down playing with all the wrapping paper, wrapping it round her own head.

Auntie Mary loves all her gifts, especially a framed photograph of her with Rosie.

Dad gets a similar photograph of us all together plus some new Levi's aftershave, etc.

I feel so happy, this is the best Christmas I've had since mum passed away.

Dad and Mary retreat to the kitchen to carry on with the Christmas dinner, just as the doorbell rings; it is Vinny with more presents. He puts the Christmas presents down and picks up Rosie and throws her into the air and she squeals with laughter.

Eamon calls Mary and Dad back into the room. "Jesus Mary and Joseph, what now? There be no Christmas dinner at this rate," says Auntie Mary. "Oh hello Vinny, I didn't see you there, happy Christmas darling."

"Yes happy Christmas, Vinny," says Dad.

"Happy Christmas everyone. Well now, get on with it, Eamon," says Vinny, "I've got to get back home as Mum likes us all to be together for Christmas."

"Okay Vinny," says Eamon.

Eamon hands me an envelope and he says, "I was told a while back by victim support that you and me were both to be compensated financially for what happened to us. Obviously my pay-out is more for the obvious reasons, so now open your envelope."

I open the envelope, inside is a letter and also a cheque for £6700. I am totally gobsmacked. "What the hell? How long have you known about this? I can't believe this," I say with tears in my eyes. Then I hug him.

Eamon is crying and in a wobbly voice says, "I didn't tell you about it Joey because I wasn't sure how much we would get and when we would get it and Joey, I want to thank you for saving my life that night and I can't imagine how horrible it must have been for you having to watch. I don't think I've ever told you Joey but I love you."

"And I love you, bro," I say wiping away a tear.

"Right, come on Eamon, tell Joey the other news," says Vinny.

Eamon says, "Ok Vinny. Well Joey, instead of selling from the Irish club, we're going to go ahead and get a shop and we have already found a shop on the High Street with a small flat above, which myself and Vinny will move into sometime in the future and we have put down a deposit, well myself and Vinny have put down a deposit. I've put down £45,000 and Vinnie also has put £45,000. I was happy to use all my money but Vinny wouldn't have it."

"No, I wouldn't have it, I don't want anybody to think I was taking advantage of Eamon's money," says Vinny, "And I wanted us to be equally responsible, so Joey we are going to open the Irish shop and you are also going to be a partner and hopefully you can make the bread, etcetera.

"I will carry on working for the time being as I'm earning good money doing these refurbishments and I've got five lads and my Dad working for me and I've got three new contracts, so I have to take on more men and Jack, if you want to change your job there's an opening with me for a ganger man and it's good money."

"Thanks Vinny. I'll think about it and let you know," says Dad.

"And as regards the shop, well that's down to you and Eamon and if you want help, my younger sisters are driving me crazy wanting to help and they don't even know about the shop yet," says Vinny smiling.

And Eamon pipes up, "so happy Christmas Joey." As I look at Eamon, I can see his sparkle returning.

I hug both Vinny and Eamon, then we all hug Dad, Mary, Rosie and laughter and tears are flowing. "Dad, you didn't seem surprised by any of this so I'm guessing you already knew?"

"Yeah I did know, they ran the idea past me and they also wanted me to know about the money and I couldn't be happier for you all and I promise to help all I can starting with teaching you how to make the salt beef that I've made for us to have over Christmas so you can all have a sample."

"Right," says Vinny, "there's one last present for you Eamon, then I better make a move or otherwise I'll be in trouble, right this is getting a bit repetitive but here you go."

Eamon slowly opens the envelope and takes out a piece of paper. "What is it, Eamon?" asks Auntie Mary.

Vinnie answers Auntie Mary as Eamon is too choked up to speak, "it's a letter from a guy I met while I was doing the refurbishment of one of the warehouses that's became a recording studio.

"I played him some of Eamon's original songs and he loved them and he wants Eamon to come in when he's feeling better to have a chat with the prospect of signing to the label." We all just look at Vinny with our mouths open like goldfishes.

Eamon leaps up and hugs Vinny and kisses him in front of us all, "I can't believe that you done this for me." says Eamon.

"Well, you kept telling me how good you were, so I thought I better get a second opinion as I'm a bit biased," and Vinny winks at us all.

"Well, I kept telling you that I was good," Eamon says laughing, "and this proves it," and he winks at us as well. "This truly is the best Christmas ever," Eamon shouts.

"Right, I really need to head off or mum will string me up, happy Christmas to you all."

Mary fetches Vinny's coat, hat and scarf and gives them to him and then she heads off to the kitchen with Dad. Eamon sees Vinny to the door, telling him to call round later.

Just as Vinny has closed the front gate, the snow is falling faster, when a large black 4x4 pulls up opposite. Eamon closes the front door and we go into the sitting room discussing our futures and I am getting Rosie dressed in her coat, hat and gloves and wellies to go out into the snow for the first time.

And then the doorbell rings.

The End